The Corner
of My Eye

The Corner

of My Eye

poetry, essays, & short stories

Vaughn F. Keller

Riverhaven Books

www.RiverhavenBooks.com

The short stories are works of fiction. The characters, events, and locales are products of the author's imagination or are used fictitiously and any resemblance to actual persons, living or dead, events, or locales is purely coincidental. Poems are poems. As for the essays, no offense is meant – in most situations.

Copyright© 2017 by Vaughn Keller

Published in the United States by
Riverhaven Books,
www.RiverhavenBooks.com

ISBN: 978-1-937588-77-9

Printed in the United States of America
by Country Press, Lakeville, Massachusetts

Designed and Edited by
Stephanie Lynn Blackman
Whitman, MA

Preface

There are wild turkeys out in the front yard and my cockapoo Jake does not approve of their presence. I saw them out of the corner of my eye before Jake announced that they were there. I know there is a poem or an essay in this scene, and I am sure Robert Frost would have found a way to use the English language to turn the bloody turkeys and my barking dog into art.

I have nothing to say about the turkeys, at least nothing nice or meaningful. They are a messy pain for suburban New Englanders.

On occasion, though, I do see things out of the corner of my eye that catch my attention and become important to me. Sometimes it is a conversation or driving by a restaurant that makes me pause. Many of these pieces began that way. Others, like sailing to Bermuda in between storms and hurricanes, were full frontal encounters – anything but out of the corner of my eye.

Whatever the impetus to get some words down, I hope you find some of these pieces to your liking and you won't think of all of them the same as Jake and I think of the turkeys in the yard.

Table of Contents

November Journal

It's the last day of October 1991. I am splurging, or binging, depending upon one's point of view and commitment to any one of a number of twelve- step programs. I am having a hot fudge sundae at an ice cream parlor in Fairfield, Connecticut. The rationale is that this is the last goodie I will have available to me for at least two weeks. It's ridiculous, but I do it anyway.

Outside it's blowing hard and raining. There are gale warnings as far south as Cape Hatteras. There is an enormous winter storm battering the East Coast. The reports of giant seas are terrifying, up to seventy feet. Boulders have been deposited in George Bush's Kennebunkport living room. He was well coached in reporting it, though, and appeared appropriately unassuming and was concerned about everyone else.

Someplace off of Bermuda there is a hurricane called Grace, and Grace is wandering rather than staying on a nice predictable storm track. So much for this two-week window of opportunity I've been telling people about. This statistical window between the end of hurricane season and the beginning of the winter storms doesn't seem to exist. Right now I am wondering if I actually heard about this "window" from a reputable source or conjured it up to ease my own mind.

There will be three of us on board *Skye*: Don MacNary, his wife Julie Wright MacNary, and me. Our plan is to sail from Norfolk, Virginia, to Saint Thomas in the American Virgin Islands. We will be going in a flotilla called the *Caribbean 1500* to honor the 1,500 miles we will be sailing. There may be more than twenty boats in the flotilla. Last year the fleet got badly beaten up during the first week of the voyage: one boat capsized, another lost a rudder. Don sent me an article describing the event from the magazine *Cruising World*. While there were some lovely pictures of the fleet arriving in St. Thomas, what stuck in my mind, however, were the boat that capsized and the lost rudder.

We are off to a difficult start. It is not just the weather. Don and Julie were alone bringing the boat from Cape May to Norfolk. As they made their way down the Chesapeake Bay, Don developed a kidney stone. He was in intense pain and Julie had to call upon the Coast Guard for help. The stone did not pass easily, and Don was in agony until a surgical intervention was made. This was not sufficient to raise doubts in my mind about this enterprise.

A few days later, still on their way down the Chesapeake, Don and Julie met two days of fog. The radar on *Skye* decided this was the right time to die. Exhausted that night, they anchored. The anchor rope felt it was the right time to wrap around the keel and saw itself through.

This was still not a sufficient prologue to the voyage. Don's son called to say that his wife had moved out and wanted a divorce. He was hurting. Julie called to tell me all of this and say that she wasn't sure we were going.

A week later, she called again to say we were .

I am wrestling with my own demons. I will be returning home to get divorced. It is very hard. Sitting here with my hot fudge sundae, I feel lost and anxious – thus my last treat with appropriate rationale.

I have bought the things I need for the voyage. I now own *Practical Sailor* magazine's best-rated safety harness and wet-weather gear. Some of my gear are gifts from my children and friends at my fiftieth birthday party last April.

I know that Don and Julie have the boat ready. They have been preparing for months. They have been reading for months. They have been talking to people for months. For Julie and me, this will be our first time offshore. Don has done several Bermuda races, but those were on larger boats with much larger crews. This is his first time skippering for this long a voyage with this green a crew. As Julie told me a couple of weeks ago, "This is the biggest adventure of our lives." Me too!

The sundae doesn't tell me why I am doing this. I've admitted to myself and others that I'm scared. Now I feel like I have to go. Up until now, the idea of this voyage was compelling. How dare I not go? My mother says I have saltwater in my veins. She likes to categorize people with metaphors. My former father-in-law (from marriage number one) fabricated that he had been in the Bermuda race. He hadn't. I plan on having pictures to prove my daring. There is some rite of passage present. I think this is true for all three of us. Don talks about it the least – at least to me.

Friday, November 1, 1991: Norfolk

We are ready. The radar has been fixed. The anchor has been taken in from the bow, stowed in the port sail locker, and returned to the bow as being the safer position for it. The riggers provided by the flotilla organizers have gone over the boat and given us a B+. The weatherman has been slightly wrong. The wind is down and it is raining lightly.

Weathermen and sailors think differently. They dress differently too. The weatherman was the only one in the formal hotel conference room with a tie on as all of the crews gathered for the pre-race briefing.

"The tropics have been quiet for the last three months. There have only been six named storms rather than the usual eight." Six rather than eight and Grace is out there with an uncertain track. This is quiet?

Six weeks ago at Center Harbor on the coast of Maine we waited for one of those six named storms, "Bob," to arrive. The crew at the Brooklin Boat Yard pulled all of the Beetle Cats out of the water. People worked together to get the dinghies up onto Ben Emory's front lawn. I stripped the sails, boom, and rudder off my 21-foot San Juan *Marking* and added scope to her mooring line. My about to be ex-wife Linda and our daughter Sarah came from where they were staying on Deer Isle to wait out the storm with the rest of us – me, my daughter Rebecca, and my son-in-law Craig – in Center Harbor. Rebecca and I fought over how anxious one should get anticipating a hurricane. Not yet thirty, my daughter has a distant relationship to fear. For sailors it only takes one storm.

The destruction of "Bob" along Cape Cod and Rhode Island was extensive. Boats were stacked like kindling along the seawalls. Up in Maine, we had but a bad wind storm with a series of squalls.

"The tropics have been quiet for the last three months." Tell that to "Bob." I wondered what was waiting for us now. The weatherman in the tie assured us that it would be a benign system for the next week. This, though, was a two-week voyage, at best.

Steve Black, organizer of the event, scheduled the 1500 a week later this year. He was pumped up telling us about how he made the decision to schedule a later departure this year when he heard the weather report. He was as excited as an NFL tailback dancing a jig in the end zone. He was sure that by delaying a week he had scored one for this year's flotilla. After what happened to the fleet last year, I can understand his exuberance.

I trust *Skye*. *Skye* is a 35-foot Camper Nicholson built in the seventies. She is a cruising boat, strongly built. She is also one of the smallest boats in the fleet. It helps that at the Stamford Boat Show in October I mentioned to boat builder Tom Morris that I was going on the trip. He asked what kind of boat and, when I told him a 35-foot Camper, Nicholson said, "Great boat." Tom is a boat builder of note and builds my dream boats in Southwest Harbor, Maine. Every time I indulge myself in a win-the-lottery fantasy, ordering a boat from Tom is first thing on the agenda. His praise of *Skye* was reassuring.

This year about twenty boats will set sail for the Caribbean as part of our flotilla. Others will take the intercoastal waterway to Florida then go across to the Bahamas, down the Bahamian chain of islands and eventually to the Virgins. They, too, have an organized event but it will take them much longer to reach their destination. We consider ourselves a cut above these intercoastal folks. We are blue water sailors. And, after all, we have jackets that say Caribbean 1500. T-shirts from last year are available too.

Tonight at the reception of wine, beer, cheese, and crackers, there was a festive atmosphere It was as though we were partying before a simple around-the-buoys race in the morning.

All of the lectures, parties, inspections, and jackets didn't diminish my anxiety. The piano player at the bar sent out lively rag tunes across the harbor as we tried to get to sleep. It was nice to hear them. After a while, though, I wanted him to stop. Sleep doesn't come easily. I know that this is the last time for many days that the bunk will be this still beneath me.

Saturday, November 2, 1991

The 136-foot long *Bill of Rights* is docked on the outboard side of the marina. Based on the design of an 1856 coastal schooner *Wanderer*, *Bill of Rights* is now used as a training vessel for various groups. She is beautiful, and I fantasize sailing south on her.

My family tree, on my father's side, reaches back to

the captain of a coastal schooner who sailed from New York to Maine. Coming down the years, my grandfather built and sailed boats in Long Island Sound. My father raced Star boats before the days of fiberglass, Dacron, and Mylar. I remember back four years ago when I took my father, my brother, and my son cruising for a week on the Chesapeake. We stopped at Annapolis and watched the middies shape up in their mid-day ritual. Looking at *Bill of Rights* I think about my father and wonder who that long ago captain was, his grandfather.

I am aware that we are going offshore. This is no coastal trip. When I was quite young I read a book about a boy who was a seafarer. He was careful, though, to point out he was a green water man. So am I, I think to myself. I am a coastal sailor, a green water man, used to bays, rivers, buoys, lighthouses, and the sight of land. An acquaintance and a friend of his climbed into and out of the Grand Canyon in a day to celebrate their fiftieth birthdays. I know that this is some kind of rite of passage for me. Sailing a 35-foot boat offshore for 1500 miles in November is different and I need to do it now while I can.

To middle-aged sailors the sailing magazines are like harlequin romances to young girls. The romance of sailing and cruising is extolled. The living through of the daily problems and sometime disasters is overlooked or set in such a glorified context that the human anxiety is placed in the background. I thank God that the kidney stone chose two weeks ago to make an appearance rather than a week from now.

Melville understood:

Whenever I find myself growing grim about the mouth; whenever it is a damp, drizzly November in my soul; whenever I find myself involuntarily pausing before coffin warehouses, and bringing up the rear of every funeral I meet; and especially whenever my hypos get such an upper hand of me that it requires a strong moral principle to prevent me from deliberately stepping into the street and methodically knocking people's hats off, then I account it high time to get to sea as soon as I can.

I am not ready to step into the street and methodically knock people's hats off but, like Ishmael, it is a damp drizzly November in my soul as I take my troubled heart to sea. Does a white whale await us?

Don plots out the Gulf Stream from the weatherman's latest coordinates -- over a week old. Where to cross this mysterious wanderer? Where will it be? What will it be like when we get there? If the wind is from the North, as it is now, we could sail into a very confused and choppy sea as the current and wind fight it out for prominence. Our neighbors in the marina on Iolanthe have just left.

1850 Hours

No wind. We've been motoring since 1400.

The first two hours of the race were exciting. The wind was light for the downwind start and we kept up with the bigger boats thanks to our spinnaker. Now it hangs, useless. We take it down and stow it below.

Don and Julie had squabbled over the course, tension

squabble, second guessing. His racing head took over. The night before he had been relaxed, saying, "I don't care at all about the race part of this." But when there are boats on either side of you and a gun goes off, it is hard not to respond. I understand. Put me anywhere near another sailboat of comparable size and I am adjusting sheets to eke out another fraction of a knot. At one point Julie held her head in her hands collecting herself.

The wind is gone. We dutifully logged the time we started our engine. In some ways it is good that the wind died. It ends the race for us. We laugh about it. After all, the racing part of this is voyage is simply an additive. The purpose of going in flotilla is safety and to enhance the enjoyment of the event, not to get cutthroat. However, when you've been brought up coaxing speed out of a boat, it is hard to give it up, especially with other boats in sight. By morning we will be alone.

I know I've changed as a skipper and think of the apologies I've given my family for the tension I created as I raced. Racing sailboats brings about all kinds of craziness. The demands for perfection by crew members becomes intolerable at times. And then there is the blaming of crew members for the mistakes of the skipper. That my family ever crewed for me is a wonder.

It is a clear starry night with a dramatic festival of lightning shooting off to the southeast and then the east of us. We speculate that these are squalls rolling up the Gulf Stream. Later we found out we were wrong. It was the remnants of a nasty low system that our friendly weatherman forgot to include in his benign designation.

Monday, November 4, 1991

Yesterday was a combination day. Periodically we would have winds gusting 20 to 30 knots and a confused sea. Julie found it frightening to be on watch at night in that kind of weather. I didn't, which surprised me. My usual mode of behavior is to stuff the tension in a macho mockery of nonchalance: "I've been through this before." This time I truly was comfortable as we rolled, slammed, and bounced about.

Nevertheless, machoman was green on Sunday. I put a patch on behind my ear, a half patch at first but was up to a full patch within a short period of time. I was lucky. We had a stretch of no-wind for the hours immediately after the patch went on. It did its job and I found myself moving comfortably with the motion without cursing the need to eat and drink. Reports come in from the other boats battling Mal de Mer. One boat eventually turned back because of the sickness of the crew.

We checked in on the flotilla radio net twice a day, morning and evening. Mostly we'd report technical stuff: positions and weather. It's at 1300 that more human interaction takes place. Before we left, we arranged to check in with *Iolanthe* and *Free as Air* in addition to the pre-set flotilla reporting. Both boats are about our size – a Creelock 37 and a Passport 37 – and are crewed by couples. It is human contact time: contact with people beyond the confines of our boat and the seemingly endless vistas of sea and sky that are our existence for days now.

We follow the ritualistic laws of gender. The three

women staff the radios and exchange the human information – beyond the technical. Everyone comments on the display of lightning, the motion, and the erratic winds. Then the men get on and talk about weather, courses, and lack of wind.

Last night the wind deserted us totally. We kept trying different combinations of tacks but finally gave in to the futility and acceptance of being becalmed and that slatting about was doing the rigging and sails potential harm without generating any forward motion. We took down the sails and the three of us slept for a few hours.

Mechanical goblins made their appearance yesterday. The boom is slotted top and bottom. The bottom slot is used for eyes for the reefing system and the boom vang. The eye for the boom vang let go in the midst of a gust with a crack like a pistol being shot off. At first we couldn't figure out what the noise was. Don has now hooked up the eye for the number three reefing point to the boom vang. This will work, as long as we don't have to reef the mainsail down to the number three reefing points.

***

We finally made it to the Gulf Stream and it was magical. Warm aqua waters with Saragossa weed. Birds. And, at night, a continuous stream of white phosphorus flows back from the lee bow. I become mesmerized by it on my midnight to three watch. Brief rain squalls come through, but the rain is warm and the wind rarely gusts up past thirty. I like being in the Gulf Stream, but we have to cross it or it will drag us north towards New

England.

The birds stay with us in the stream. One can't seem to get its "solid" legs and slips off the boom when it tries to perch. We tried handouts of food to retain their interest, but they left for their own journey and again we are alone. We haven't seen any other boats since our first night out of Norfolk.

The weather has created a dilemma. We have had hours of no wind intermixed with squalls. We are the smallest boat in the fleet. The larger boats are pulling ahead and tend to go under power whenever there is no wind. With a total of forty gallons of fuel for the 1500 miles, we are parsimonious with the use of the engine. However, ahead of us still lie the doldrums. That is where we had planned on using the fuel – not now.

Thursday, November 7, 1991

We are getting closer to Bermuda and are only one day, possibly two, from the way point at which we turn south heading towards the Virgin Islands. The route, as explained during the briefings in Norfolk, is deceptively simple: leave Norfolk, pick a point about 150 miles south of Bermuda, stay on a direct route to this way point as much as possible. However, get across the Gulf Stream quickly. When you get south of Bermuda, go due south through the doldrums and into the wonderful warm Easterlies of the trade winds. Piece of cake. Easier if there is wind.

We have been at sea now for five days with little wind. When we have had wind, it has been gusty and associated with small lows. We've done a lot of motoring and have moved eastward trying to find wind from the east. The larger boats are way ahead of us and no one has found an east wind. They have wind, but it is right on the nose from the south. Way south of us they are slamming into 30 knots of wind on the nose and 12-foot seas.

We have deliberated, re-deliberated, and deliberated again about going into Bermuda to get fuel. There *is* no wind for several hundred miles and then it is from the wrong direction. This high-pressure system that we are in is static. No wind. No sun. No fun.

On *Free As Air* Brian and Carol are going through the same set of deliberations. Brian and Don now get on the 1300 radio exchange. It is technical. Captain's business. Brian reports that this high is sufficiently strong and large enough to be affecting the trade winds. Weatherfax is a wonderful tool, but we hate the news it is bringing us.

Along the east coast of the United States all hell is breaking loose – multiple storms with gale winds. There is another fleet behind us by a few days that departed from Beaufort, North Carolina. We pick up their radio transmissions. They are getting hammered badly.

Again, I reflect on this two-week "window" of opportunity between the end of hurricane season and the beginning of the Northeast storms. A week before we left or a week later and we would have been *in* the middle of very large, very intense storms. As far as storms are concerned, we have been very lucky. The guy with the tie was right. We are in the midst of this benign, very static high. The problem is we also have no wind. Don had been right. When we left the briefing I said, "That sounds great." He replied, "There may be no wind." I'm learning about weather systems. This is very different from coastal cruising. Actually, it is not. It is simply different from the haphazard way I have done coastal cruising. When ports are nearby, the only thing I have ever worried about were hurricanes and fog. No wind, you motored and tanked up. There's no place out here to tank up.

***

Of the three of us, Don is the only one who seems to have fallen into a comfortable sleep pattern. I had read a few articles about watches before we left, and we are following a system that I abstracted from these articles. The core concept is that we humans need one period of uninterrupted sleep a day of at least six hours so we can get sufficient R.E.M. sleep – to dream, perchance to dream – or we go bonkers. The second notion is that between the hours of 6 and 9 P.M. no one really sleeps. The third is that the cook should have a different schedule than the others because of the need to feed the crew three or four times a day.

Our plan was to rotate cooking duties. So Julie began as cook. From 6 to 12 A.M. Don had the watch. I came on from 12 to 6. Lunch would be sandwiches. We would eat dinner about 5:30. Julie would be on watch from 6 to 9. Don or I would clean up from dinner, then Don would go on watch from 9 to 12. I would do 12 to 3. Julie would do 3 to 6. I was the only one without a night time six-hour sleep period because of the bloody 12-3 watch. I was beat.

It did not work out as planned. Julie cooked throughout the voyage. Figuring out how that happened would be a dissertation. My guess is that it was a combination of gender expectations, experience sailing, and, perhaps most importantly, she had also stowed the food and knew where everything was.

Don and I both felt comfortable standing the watches without much of a sense of backup. Julie did not. Night watches are especially uncomfortable for her. No, non-sailing friends, you don't anchor at night.

Tonight Don and I are switching watches. Sleep, dear delicious wonderful sleep. Morpheus, right now you are my favorite god.

***

We are visited by beautiful black and white birds with long tails. Julie looks them up in her bird book and tells us that they are tropic birds. They are native to Bermuda and carry a different name there.

We are trailing a fishing line. Some of the other boats claim they have caught fish. I have seen a few flying fish and one other that I couldn't name. Fresh fish would be wonderful. We are eating well, but somehow fresh fish would be delightful.

The water and air temperature are warm. I am struck most by the color of the water. It is a rich cobalt blue, unlike anything I have ever seen. I understand more fully now the distinction between a green-water man and a blue-water man.

This is so different from the murky greenish gray of Long Island Sound, or even the clear gray of the Gulf of Maine. It is magnificently clean and pure. At times I want to scoop it up and throw it over me, almost to embrace it. At night, the phosphorous is still with us even though we are no longer in the Stream. I wonder whether that is true throughout the oceans of the world.

***

Being alone on the late-night watch is an invitation to my personal demons to join me. Alternating cascades of love and rage stretch out as I contemplate the end of the voyage and the return home. They are the most intense as the watch begins and then subside as if rocked away by the motion of the boat. Eventually an easier emotional rhythm sets in and sleep comes easily at three in the morning.

***

From a Bermuda radio station we learn that a major gale is expected. It is not mentioned by the stateside weather service. Which do we pay attention to? We hope to be south of any major weather system in a few days.

***

A small freighter passed close to us today. We watched him from a distance make circles. He then headed for us on a collision course. We tried to hail him several times on channel sixteen, but he didn't answer. Finally he answered and cryptically told us to hold course and speed. Concerned about the radar image we made with our reflector, we asked him how well he could see us on his scope. He replied that his radar wasn't on. Given his tone of voice, I didn't think he was the kind of person strangers asked favors of. It was a very strange encounter that left me with a host of explanations any one of which could have given birth to a mystery novel.

Friday, November 8, 1991

Last night Don and I exchanged watches. I got to sleep from 12 to 6. Wrong. I don't even remember what time it was. I do know that my all-too-corporeal self was having a difficult time staying in the pilot berth even with its relatively high side. I would try to sleep and just start to fall into a deep sleep when *Skye* would rock violently in the building squall. I hung on. Unlike an animal, I can't hang on and sleep at the same time. My beautiful anticipation of a long sleep in the dark was disappearing. I opened my eyes and realized that neither Don nor Julie were asleep in the port settee berth. Then I heard, "Vaughn, we need help."

It's the noise. In a strong squall the wind is an erratic instrument, sometimes moaning, sometimes shrieking. In the dark it can be terrifying. On deck the tones change quickly as the sails and shrouds slam about relative to the direction of the storm. We were being buffeted by one gust after another. We were first tipped over to one side, would come back up, and then be pushed over again.

Organization paid off. I knew where my wet weather

gear and harness were in the wet locker. Only my jacket. The pants and boots would take too long. Topsiders would do.

Don shouted, "Get the foredeck light." I wish I'd memorized the electrical panel. *Skye* was still new to me and she and I were moving in different directions as I tried to find the right light. It was like reading tiny street signs from an elevated train. I got it.

Good, the drop boards weren't in. One less obstacle to get on deck. Halfway through the companionway a gust hit and *Skye* rolled to leeward. I was pinned for a minute against the side.

Pulling myself into the cockpit, I heard the water rolling from the bow, down the deck, and over the cabin top behind me. It was coming too fast for me to do anything about it. Up and over the dodger it came and, oh shit, down over my wet weather jacket and down drenching my sweatpants.

"Take the wheel," Don shouted. What glorious words. I love you oh captain, my captain. You are going forward on this bucking bronco to reef the mainsail. You are going to deal with the infinitely patient task of wrestling the mainsail down to reef it while all I have to do is keep this twisting, jumping hunk of fiberglass and wood headed in a direction that doesn't throw us into a jibe, a tack, or some other disaster.

The foredeck light makes the boat eerie. The light shows the sheets of rain and spindrift coming off the waves. We are in a small cocoon of light, twisting in response to waves we only see when they have control of us.

At Don's direction, Julie eases the main and the noise escalates with the luffing sail trying to rip itself apart. It's Don's boat. He's sailed it for three years. He's moved forward on pitching decks for more than forty years. He did it. Nothing broke. Nothing got fouled. The reef is in and we are underway. "What a difference a reef makes, twenty-four lonely…" I do this silliness with lyrics when I get tense. It drives my youngest daughter Sarah nuts. I keep explaining to her that it is the duty of fathers to embarrass their eleven-year-old daughters.

I never got my six hours of uninterrupted sleep. Julie took a picture of me the next day to prove it.

***

Fuel has continued to be a concern, but finally a decision has been made. We are going to Bermuda. The boats immediately ahead of us continue to encounter light southerly winds. Father on down they are experiencing heavy southerly winds. Over the radio Brian and Don exchange theories supporting continuing on, then Bermuda, then St. Thomas again. At one point Brian lays out his weather analysis and the three of us are sure he is leading up to say he is going to Bermuda. He doesn't. We laugh, breaking the tension.

It has been a very slow trip so far, and with the continued forecast of light airs I am beginning to worry about my time. I have to return to work to run a new workshop. The combination predicted light winds and fuel concerns lead us to Bermuda. Finally, a decision. We all feel lighter about it.

Consequently, the Atlantic turned on a perfect day. We had sun, sustained sun. It blew 20 knots all day as we flew towards Bermuda on an easy broad reach. This was fun. This was the way I had imagined the two weeks would be. Silly me.

I am excited about going there. I'm glad the decision has been made. Bermuda is a new place for me. It may be that my coastal-cruising genes have been reactivated. Oh, a shower, a hot delicious wonderful shower, and a bunk that doesn't move, and sleeping through the night.

***

Julie saw land first. I don't know what I had expected, but I was surprised by the very narrow opening that comprises the entrance to St. George's Harbor. Any more than two boats would have a difficult time squeezing through the coral cut that separates the harbor from the ocean. Fortunately the entrance is very well buoyed.

Customs officials in Bermuda have to be the most polite customs people I have encountered. Not only were they efficient and pleasant, they actually made us feel welcome. It went quickly and soon we were at anchor and pumping up the dinghy to go ashore.

Free As Air was right behind us, coming through the cut and lay outboard of us for the customs inspection. It was late afternoon and the notion of land and someone else cooking and cleaning dominated our thoughts. Off came the patches from behind our ears.

We might have been better leaving them on. There is no floating dinghy dock at St. Georges. Instead, there are steps cut into the sea wall. You unload, climb up the steps, and walk your dinghy down the wall to make room for others at the steps. This all works quite well if you haven't just come in from six days at sea. The inner ear does not like changes. My brain was convinced we were still moving up and down as I tried to maneuver on land. Now I was land sick.

We did make it the twenty or so yards to the White Horse Saloon without falling down. Never has a pint of beer tasted so good nor have the chicken wings disappeared so fast as when Brian and Carol, Don and Julie, and I got to the White Horse.

Sunday, November 10, 1991

I am in love with Bermuda. I have moved ashore to get some work done on a class I am taking. I also need some privacy to be with myself.

I am staying at Hillcrest House which is owned and run by Mrs. Tru Robinson. She is a lovely lady in her eighties who at one point in her life sailed in a schooner from England to India.

The room I am in is small but clean. The building itself has the facade of a Southern Plantation. It sits high on top of a hill overlooking the harbor. I have rented a moped to see Bermuda and have arranged to fly back to New York on Tuesday at noon.

Friday night I slept on board and delighted in the luxury of waking slowly and gradually with no chores that simply had to get done. After helping me get settled at Hillcrest, Don and Julie went in search of a laundromat. For the three of us, the rest of Saturday was devoted to arrangements.

There is a frog on Bermuda, species unknown to me, that is the loudest creature I have ever heard. It loves the nighttime. I am used to New England crickets. These frogs are four times as loud. They do not make a pleasant sound. I questioned at first if I would be able to sleep. I should have known better. Sleep came easily, deeply, and was wonderfully long. The bed did not move. The rhythm of living on land was returning.

***

It was good to ride the moped. Eleven years ago I gave up my motorcycle days. My daughter Sarah was born, and I agreed to give up riding as an act of responsible parenting. Still, I miss the freedom and the moped brought the memories back.

I have especially missed riding on a warm summer night aware of the differences in temperatures going up and down hills. The smells change with foliage, restaurants, and the water, and it is a feast for the senses. It was a treat to ride again, even on a moped.

***

Julie is amazing. She is one of those people who everyone loves. She has this capacity to be both straightforward and accepting at the same time. She is devoid of guile and artifice. So, of course, she has stayed friends with her former in-laws and, by coincidence, her former brother-in-law and his wife are here on Bermuda this week.

Redwood Wright is a trustee of the Bermuda Marine

Station and is here for a meeting. We had dinner with Red and his wife Mary last night. It was delightful.

Monday, November 11, 1991

We monitor the radio net for news about the boats that continued on to St. Thomas. *Iolanthe* burned out its alternator in clouds of black smoke. It sounds like the master switch was thrown in the wrong position when the engine was running. The fleet has continued to get hit with 20 to 30 knots of winds out of the south as they beat their way to Saint Thomas.

Seas are in the 12-foot range and equipment and people are beginning to break. Here, in Bermuda, we speculate what it must be like now on the fifth day of that weather and express gratitude that it is not us.

Golden Odyssey has lost its head stay. It continues on without the use of a mainsail. The mast is being supported by the luff of the jib and the jury rigging of halyards. This is the first voyage for the owners on their new boat.

Another boat has lost its main and goes under jib and jigger while they repair the main. *Morning Star*, a fifty-foot Hinckley, has decided it has had enough pounding to weather and has altered course to come back to Bermuda.

We speculate about the "lemming" effect. Why haven't more boats decided, "The hell with this," and altered course for Bermuda where they could wait out this unusual Southerly until a favorable Easterly sets in? The fatigue on people must be significant at this point.

Several of the boats sail with short crews.

There is a double-edged sword to this notion of a flotilla. My reading comes into play as I recall Irving Janis's book <u>Groupthink</u>. There can be an illusion of invulnerability because of the presence of the group. You believe it makes things safer if you get in trouble; but it also convinces you that nothing can happen to you as long as you stay with the group. Independent critical thinking is surrendered for "groupthink.

A less organized fleet left Beaufort, North Carolina a few days after we left Norfolk. They got hit first by the storm that rolled up the Eastern Seaboard and then ran into the Southerlies. Some of the boats from that fleet are now making their way to Bermuda rather than continuing on south.

Last night at dinner on board *Skye*, we listened to channels 16 and 68 on VHF. A United States Coast Guard plane and harbor radio Bermuda patiently and professionally offered assistance to one of the boats from the Beaufort fleet that was struggling to make it to Bermuda.

The 41-foot boat was home built by the skipper who was single handing it to the Virgin Islands. He had been without sustained sleep for nine days. Again, we indulged in questions and speculations. Why doesn't he heave to and get some sleep? Does he know how? Is he too tired to make these adjustments?

Bermuda Search and Rescue has only one boat capable of engaging in an offshore rescue attempt. It was down for repairs. Only their small boat was available, and we heard the skipper say he was only willing to go out into those seas if it was a matter of life or death.

Increasingly I am convinced of the folly of flotilla sailing. I believe it has become an attractive option for people who do not have the experience to sail offshore alone. The flotilla conveys a safety net that it in fact does not have. There is no flotilla leader or crash boat. There is no one with the charge of interpreting the weather and making recommendations. Everyone sails at their own pace, so the boats only stay together for the first day or so. The bigger boats quickly separate from the smaller boats. No one talks about the suppression of critical judgment that takes place.

I'm deeply impressed with the professionalism of the Coast Guard pilot as he tries to work with the exhausted skipper of the home-made yacht. He even gives him an abbreviated verbal mental status exam to determine how severe the fatigue is. The skipper cannot count up to ten. I leave *Skye* that night not knowing what happened to the exhausted skipper.

***

The morning had been especially lovely. Red and Mary took us on a tour of the Bermuda Marine station. I am so enamored with the place that I begin to think about holding one of our conferences there.

Following the tour, we watched a parade in Saint George's. It is Remembrance Day, Veteran's Day in the United States. We watched the parade from the steps of the cathedral.

Late Monday

Morning Star is in. Another boat on the way to St. Thomas has run into trouble. It lost its mast. The coast guard is tracking its progress back to Bermuda.

The lone skipper in his home-made craft made it in. The coasties showed up to have their picture taken with the exhausted single-handing skipper.

We had an opportunity to talk with the flight crew and the skipper. The rescue plane had been in the air too long and eventually had to stand down at the naval air station. But they continued talking to him.

We chatted about the C130 and its role as an air-sea rescue platform. They talked about hundreds of people dying at sea right now, refugees from Haiti leaving in small overcrowded boats. We extolled the virtues of the global positioning system, and even the skipper of the home-built boat thought he might break down and get one.

I asked him why he hadn't taken time to heave to and get some sleep. He said he wanted to keep up with the fleet. He only had a VHF radio and didn't want to be out of touch with the others. Again, the illusion of invulnerability. He had set off for the Virgin Islands alone without GPS, without Loran, without charts for Bermuda, and without knowing celestial navigation. (He was going to teach himself underway.) He had an EPIRB (an emergency system that sends out a radio signal) but no batteries for it. He had a VHF radio (only useful to the horizon) but no SSB radio (Single Side Band which can transmit around the globe), so his communications were limited.

I found myself becoming sympathetic to those who believe that the U.S. Coast Guard should present a bill for services rendered. He had cost the taxpayers thousands of dollars because of his negligence.

***

The skipper of one of our fleet who came in to Bermuda is distraught. His boat is too big for the young skipper to take on alone to the islands. His wife has been seriously ill, and he'd promised her and their children Thanksgiving in the Caribbean. He has his business to attend to. His crew, friends, need to get back to their lives. He wants to go on.

He was tempted, so tempted that he came to the customs dock to begin clearance. His plan was to slug it out under power into 12- to 15-foot seas for a day or two and hope the Easterlies would come in. Wisdom overcame obsession and I see him on the phone making airline reservations.

Tuesday, November 12, 1991

I promised to call Glen, Don's dad, when I got home and tell them that *Skye* would be leaving Bermuda that afternoon. *Skye*'s ETA at Saint Thomas is November 20th, eight days from now. Waving good-bye from the concrete pier I wished I was going with them.

***

I've been feeling low all morning. I don't want to go home to deal with rebuilding my life at fifty. The stay in Bermuda had lifted the bleakness of November, if only for a few days.

The young skipper of the other boat sits behind me as we fly towards New York. A professional crew will take his boat to the islands. He watched it sail off without him. He is a nice man, torn between obligations and the sultry siren call of the Caribbean. I think about his wife, her battle, and his hope for her to join him once the boat gets to the islands.

I know the dream. The warm tropical waters can be healing in a way that is truly unique.

The first time I experienced this was in the Abacos. I had been operated on and radiated for cancer. My then wife was newly pregnant with Sarah. I was still weak from the onslaught of the radiation treatment. The purple ink they used to paint the radiation target area rubbed off on everything: shirts, sheets, anything that touched my trunk. The tattoo marks indicating the outer limits of the radiation field would be with me forever.

For six weeks the nausea would come, conditioned, the instant the elevator door opened and I smelled the new carpeting of the nuclear medicine waiting room. The bad retching would begin an hour after the treatment while I rode the train back to Westport from New York. I got used to riding in filthy restrooms, dry-heaving up a metallic tasting nothing.

The Abacos were hot in August, but they restored me. I had my older children and my new wife with me and four weeks to heal. Four weeks to let the warm green water work its magic.

It did. I'm drawn back to the young skipper and the

unknown health battles that he and his wife are struggling with. I hope they make it south for Thanksgiving.

***

We fasten our seat belts as the 727 loses altitude on its approach to Kennedy. Within minutes I will walk through the terminal doors to the noise of New York and the now unfamiliar chill of mid-November. Before I leave I will call Glen and let him know that *Skye* is on her way south to the islands.

The New House
for Melody

There were four bushes along the road.
"I'd probably pull them out," she said.
"Maybe I should trim them," he said.
"Let's wait," she said.
And they did
Until the first Monday after their first
Weekend together and she pointed out
The new blooms and all the buds
On the four Rose of Sharon trees.
Later he watched her,
Watering can in hand,
Looking at the blooms.

Eulogy
for a Political Mother

Some of the people who have written about Mom divide her life into three segments: before she entered politics, her political career, and then after politics. Don't believe it. There was just before and after. I know. I was there when it all changed.

She had been upstairs reading, sitting in that old chair that had been a hand-me-down from my great-grandfather. It was late afternoon. Dad wasn't home from work yet. My sisters were watching their allowable one-hour allotment of TV a day. I had just come home from high school track practice and was making myself a peanut butter and jelly sandwich. Or, as she would say, "spoiling my supper."

Suddenly she ran downstairs, book in hand. "Wait until you hear this," she said. "You've got to hear this." Like I had a choice. And she read. She read a quotation which she would repeat over and over again, eventually from memory. I guarantee every member of my family and many of you now know it by heart because you have heard it so many times. So, bear with me; here it is, one more time:

Power without love is reckless and abusive, and love without power is sentimental and anemic. Power, at its best, is love implementing the demands of justice, and justice, at its best, is power correcting everything that stands against love.

It was 1967. As I now know, it was from Reverend Doctor Martin Luther King's last book, *Where Do We Go From Here: Chaos or Community.*

Anyone who doubts that a book can change someone's life didn't know my mother. Before she read that book she was a mother, a wife, a history teacher. After that book, well, suffice it to say that there was more chaos than community in our house. My mother didn't enter politics; she became political. After that book friends and politicians of the liberal persuasion got divided into two camps: there were those who were judged to be well meaning but "anemic and sentimental" and then there were those, the ones she respected, who "implemented the demands of justice."

After that book she became a student of power, and she was determined to use whatever power she could muster to make things better. Unlike many of her colleagues, making things better was not necessarily focused on those of us who lived and worked in her district. For her, making things better was global, universal: "Love implementing the demands of justice" and "Power correcting everything that stands against love."

That book changed not only her life, it changed ours. She decided to run for political office: First the state legislature, and later congress. My father, my sisters, and I saw our home become transformed into campaign headquarters on more than one occasion. It all depended on how well the fundraising was going. We licked envelopes, made signs, and did all of the other things that are called for when one's mother is determined to change the world. Many of you were there with us. Some of you met her after the early campaigns, when there were real campaign headquarters.

Eventually the newspapers started calling her a "politician." She hated being called a politician. "I am a representative," she would say. As with many things, that would be said with passion and an understanding that reached way beyond what most reporters and many of her colleagues would ever grasp.

Dad has said that politics broke her heart. Certainly she had her disappointments, and some of the people she'd supported failed to live up to their promise and promises. In the Sermon on the Mount, Jesus included this beatitude: "Blessed are they that hunger and thirst after <u>justice</u>: for they shall have their fill."

"Have their fill." My mother? Let's face it: when it came to justice, Mom was ravenous. We all know what she accomplished, and it is significant. But her fill? During this past decade she spent a lot of time on college campuses and laid out a grand list of things she considered to be the unfinished agenda of this country and our world. She would have gratefully accepted a little more filling.

Two months ago she asked me to drive her to Northeast State for still one more lecture in still one more college lecture series. I hadn't heard her speak in a few years, so I was delighted when she invited me to drive her. On the drive up we talked about the family and how we were all doing. She provided me with a complete analysis of the party and its current successes, failures, and personalities. We also talked a bit about her frustration at the lack of political energy she was detecting on college campuses. She had talked about this before, but something was changing in the way she thought about it.

I was not surprised when she opened her talk with the story of her reading *Where Do We Go From Here* and how it had transformed her. I was not surprised when she then quoted King's magnificent words about love and justice and power and talked about how meaningful those words were to her. When she ended her talk, there was a difference. It caught me up short. I was no longer her son listening to the familiar; I was a member of the audience attending to every word. It was about the transition from her world to ours, from her generation to mine.

She concluded with a quotation from T.S. Eliot:

"For last year's words belong to last year's language
And next year's words await another voice."

She paused. Then she said to us – to me, to you: "The world awaits another voice. Yours."

With that, she left the stage.

Triumphs

Triumphs, for most of us,
Appear to be confined
To three generations.
My parents knew
When I reached and when I refused,
When I rose and when I fell,
When I cared and when I dismissed.

My children hear stories of my past
And are polite up to the point
Where repetition invites boredom
And they excuse themselves to another task,
Another room, or a place with walls I cannot breach.

My grandchildren treat me as an artifact
From a distant past that has little to do with their lives,
An intrusion into the now of their experience –
Irrelevant, obsolete, and maybe wasteful of their time.

When I am wise, I realize I must tack
Because the wind has changed:
My memories of triumphs past are for me and friends.
My focus now is on the children I raised,
They still need my affirmations; sometimes more than ever
And the children they are raising
Even though

There are times I do not understand the fuss made
Or the lavishness of the attention given.

At times it feels sufficient to be present,
A cycle of completion,
A continuation and a passing,
A person to introduce to friends
Before hustling off to some more important
Gathering or task birthing triumphs of their own.

My children know their children as I know mine
And my parents knew me.
My own grandparents looked on
And smiled smiles as enigmatic as
Those I smile today,
The smiles of an old portrait
Hanging in the hall.
I wonder if they wonder:
"What's he smiling at?"

Paris Afternoon

We left our room on Rue Git le Cour and started walking towards the Place St. Michel. I wanted to get out of the room, to walk, and then get a coffee at the café I had visited that morning. We could sit outside. No one would notice the smell of sex from our afternoon in bed. We could shower later, before dinner.

It was an unseasonably warm April in Paris. Easter was only two days away, and a group of priests dressed in white surplices over black cassocks were walking down Boul Mich, heading towards the Seine. The lead priest held a crucifix attached to a tall poll. A procession trailed them, mostly women, older, dressed in black.

"What's that all about?" she asked.

"It's Good Friday. Probably headed to Notre Dame to do the Stations of the Cross."

"What are the Stations of the Cross?"

"Remember. I told you about them when we went to midnight Mass last year. You asked what the plaques were on the walls at the Church of the Assumption."

"Oh, yeah. I forgot. Tell me again."

"Each plaque is for a different stop as Jesus was led to be crucified."

"How many are there."

"I don't know. Ten. Twelve."

"I thought you were supposed to be Catholic."

"Yeah, right."

"I thought you were an altar boy."

"I was."

I didn't add that often I would be the one holding the crucifix in our small church as Father McCormick led the prayers for the stations. Looking at the scenes would terrify me: being whipped, having a crown of thorns pushed down onto my head, having nails driven into my feet and hands, and then a spear shoved into my side.

One Good Friday I told my mother I wanted to stop being an altar boy. She told me to talk to Father McCormick about it. I did. He told me he didn't want me to quit but I didn't have to do Good Friday anymore.

"Sometimes I wish I had a religion," she said.

"No you don't. Believe me."

"That looks sweet."

"I wouldn't call a crucifixion sweet."

"You know what I mean, the procession. All of them going together."

"No, I don't know what you mean, it's sweet."

"Forget it. Let's talk about something else."

As we found a table in front of the café, she talked about something else, "Do you think every city gives nicknames to its major streets. Commonwealth Avenue is Comm Ave. Boulevard St. Michel is Boul Mich. Even you use Boul Mich, and you've only been here for three days."

"Are you saying I'm being pretentious?"

"Thus sayest, mon amour."

"Now who's being pretentious?"

"I'm just teasing."

"I thought you didn't like teasing."

"Just when you tease me."

Our coffees came. I took out the copy of Mellow's biography of Hemingway I had bought at Shakespeare and Company when we first arrived. She had wanted to go to the d'Orsay first to see the impressionists. I wanted to sit outside Shakespeare and Company and imagine myself in a 1920s' Paris. She said what I really wanted was to be inside Woody Allen's *Midnight in Paris*.

It was a collision of college majors, art history and English, with a first trip to Paris for either one of us. I won with the argument that we were both tired from the night flight from Boston and we could go to the d'Orsay after we had lunch and naps. I had yet to open the book. Walking, lovemaking, eating, and museums had taken over time.

She tapped on my book, "You aren't going to read are you? I didn't bring anything to read. If I had known you were going to read, I would have brought something or stayed in the hotel."

"Let me read for a few minutes. Just the introduction."

"I'm going back to the hotel."

"Okay. I won't read for God's sake. Why are you so grouchy?"

"I'm not being grouchy. You're being rude, reading while I just sit here."

"Oh, come on. You read every morning at breakfast."

"That's different. I'm reading the newspaper and so

are you. It's like a ritual. It's what we do." She was smiling now. "You know it's different."

I could have acknowledged that "yes" it was different, but I was still irritated because she couldn't wait a few minutes while I read the introduction. I returned Hemingway to my backpack without responding.

We sat quietly. "What do you want to talk about," I asked.

"I don't know. I just didn't want to be sitting her like a dolt while you read."

"Okay. So, what do you want to talk about? Or should be both sit here like dolts without talking and no one reading?"

"Stop it."

"Stop what?"

"Your bullshit. You know exactly what I'm talking about."

I didn't respond. A few minutes went by while we both looked out at the people in the square. The Stations of the Cross procession had left us. By now the pilgrims would be reaching the square in front of Notre Dame. A cloud covered the early evening sun and I remembered asking Father McCormick if it always got dark in the late afternoon when Christ died. He had answered "no" and he talked about different times and weather. He went from Father McCormick to Father Mike, to Mike, to leaving the priesthood and getting married.

"Where do you want to go for dinner?" I asked.

"Is it my turn tonight?"

"Yes."

After two nights of some tussling over where to eat based on the guidebook recommendations, we had decided to take turns.

"I don't know. I didn't bring the book with me."

"If you had, you could have been figuring out where to eat and I could have been reading the introduction."

"Stop it."

"I'm only teasing."

"I hate it when you tease me. You do it all the time."

"No I don't, and it's only teasing."

I drop it without acknowledging that I know I am pushing her away. Intimacy broken; trust diminished. There is so much I don't say. So much I feel it is useless to say. So much that I have said before without any acknowledgement that I just might be right about how we fuck up our relationship or how her super sensitivity fucks it up which was more to the point. I would have settled for a "you might be right." Not right. Just "Might be right." I knew it would never happen.

My teasing is sometimes hostile, and we both knew it. She had left the dinner table a year ago at my parents' house. My family had ganged up on her with our teasing, and we had gone too far. The dinner table that should have drawn us together had become a playing field to see how separate we could possibly become and all because she didn't want to learn how to play poker. We started competing to see who could be the cleverest teaser. We did that a lot. She was the target and poker was the content.

In my family we always play poker after big family dinners. It's what we do. She didn't want to learn how. She said she didn't like poker. By that time we had been together long enough that she was no longer a "guest." We had been together long enough so I didn't stick up for her. We had been together long enough that she was fair game for the others.

"I know I tease, but you know I love you," I said.

"I don't when you tease me. You know that."

"I wouldn't care enough to tease you if I didn't love you. It's a kind of intimacy."

"Bullshit. You tease other people you don't love. Everyone in your family teases. It's hostile. You're hostile when you tease. You never put yourself down. It's always someone else."

"You're super sensitive."

"I'm going back to the hotel."

"I'm sorry."

"No you're not."

"Yes, I really am. What if we have dinner at the same place we did the first night? What was it called?"

"Osteria del Passepartout."

"What about eating there again. It was good."

"We're in Paris. I don't want to do Italian."

"You like Italian, and it was very good."

"I want to go back and look at the guide book. It's my turn to choose."

"I was just making a suggestion."

She looked across the square to the Boul Mich. No one was going up the boulevard. Everyone was coming down, heading for the bridge to Ile de la Cite and the churches.

"I know. Let's be nice to one another. We're only here for a week," she said.

"It's not much time."

"No, it's not."

"Are you finished with your coffee?" I asked.

"Almost."

"No more teasing," I promise.

"You sure?"

"Yes, you're right. We don't have much time."

It had gotten later than I had thought. Across the city the bells began to ring out the Angelus. My mother would have told me to say three Hail Marys to remind myself of the sacrifice Christ had made for my sins.

"Shall we go?" I asked.

"Are you through with your coffee?

"Yes."

"Let's walk down to the river. Maybe we'll find a place that looks good."

"Up to you. It's your turn."

"Are you teasing?"

"No."

"Sarcastic?"

"No. It's your turn. That's all. If that's what you want."

"Yes. We don't have a lot of time. Let's not waste any going back to the hotel. Tonight, let's be spontaneous. On other nights we can plan."

The bells across the city continued to ring the Angelus.

Donny Neighbor

I met Donny Hope, an old friend of mine,
In a bar at the bottom of my street
During a pause in the blizzard last week.

We stared on and off at each other
For about five minutes before Donny Hope
Finally asked if I wasn't who I was
And I said yes, I was his old neighbor.

We talked for about ten minutes more
After which time we silently agreed
That we belonged in different bars
And that the blizzard had made a mistake.

I finished my beer and said good-bye
To Donny Hope, my old friend and neighbor,
But instead of moving on to my usual bar,
I climbed back up my street in the blizzard.

Floyd, Virginia

We had promised ourselves we would travel without much of an agenda. We had chosen our twenty-one-foot Rialta RV because it was small enough to handle in restricted areas and low enough so we didn't have to worry about bridge clearances – trees maybe, but not bridges. Small as it was, it had all of the necessities: refrigerator, stove, porta potty, and bunks.

Mary Ann and I were traveling with Charley, our middle-aged miniature poodle. Charley travels well, like his namesake. You see Charley was named after another poodle, John Steinbeck's full-sized Standard who accompanied Steinbeck on his American travel adventure which he lovingly reported in *Travels With Charley.*

So there we were, at the beginning of our adventure. We decided, though, that we needed a shake down for both us and the vehicle before we took off on the big one. The "Big One" was to be a trip west to Glacier National Park on the Montana-Canada border and then follow the Rockies south, visiting all of the major national parks as we went, a six-week excursion.

How, though, would we do in a vehicle this small? Our Rialta had low miles, but it was not new. Roughly a thousand miles later, I can report that we all did very well. And we chose well for our shake-down voyage.

We hustled across Massachusetts, into New York,

and down into Pennsylvania. We were headed south. New England had given us a cold wet April, and we wanted to get to Virginia where the "real" adventure would begin.

The Blue Ridge Highway begins where Skyline Drive ends and continues for more than 450 miles until it ends at the Cherokee reservation fifty miles from Asheville, North Carolina. It is a beautiful road. It doesn't have the majesty of the Pacific Coast Highway, but the vistas of mountains, valleys, meadows, waterfalls, and farms is wonderfully eastern.

To say it is a limited-access highway is an understatement. There is no commerce allowed, and there are many, sometimes many many, miles between entrances and exits, and when these exist you may still be a long way from any commercial establishments. Adding to the remoteness, in late April the national and state campgrounds and picnic grounds were not yet open.

While our on-board porta potty was in working order, Mary Ann saw such a contraption as an emergency device, so we had relied on campground and roadside facilities and the device remained immaculately clean and unused as we traveled on down the road. The Blue Ridge Highway, though, presented a challenge.

Let's be honest. When you have to go, you have to go. The miles kept rolling by without an exit to be found. Tupper's Holler Restaurant was barely visible off on a side road that, for a short time, paralleled the highway. Of course, we had missed the exit.

"Turn around."

"Where."

"Doesn't matter. There aren't any other cars."

And so it was that I turned around in the middle of the road and headed back the mile or so to where we could get off and find relief.

We stayed for lunch and conversation. Being from Plymouth, Massachusetts, of Pilgrim fame, makes for an easy conversation starter. Our waitress, she would have laughed at calling her waitperson or server, had been to Boston and was going again next summer. She and her husband were also RV campers, which made conversation flow easily, especially when we confessed to being "newbies."

"Just retired?"

"Yes. Just bought it."

"You're going to love it. Only way to go."

One thing led to another and we asked her about the town where we had pulled off: Floyd, Virginia.

"Drive down into the valley. It's just about six miles. You'll know when you hit the center of town. Only stop light there. Interesting place."

Our first adventure. Our first "We have no agenda" stop. And what a stop it was.

Floyd is its own wonderful universe. It's small, maybe a minute to drive through, and that's a relatively slow minute. But you can't miss the galleries and the coffee shop and, in our world, that configuration demands a stop, not just a drive through. And stop we did. Then we noticed all of the signs for music. Now, remember, this is a one-minute town.

The bookstore was downstairs, the coffee shop was up. The coffee roaster was on the first floor behind the bookstore and, if they ran out of a particular flavor upstairs, it was easy to run downstairs in hopes that the desired flavor was being processed or was already bagged. Mary Ann started upstairs – coffee always came first – and I started down.

I love small bookstores. There is almost always someone to chat with, and they usually know the books they are selling as well as the town where they are selling them. This was no different. She was sitting behind the counter reading. She offered help. I replied I was in browse mode. She returned to her reading.

I noticed a lot of books about music and a good many of them were about bluegrass. So I asked her. She smiled. "You're on the Crooked Road."

"The Crooked Road. What's the Crooked Road."

"From a bit north of here to the coal areas. Route 58. More music – country and bluegrass mostly – than anyplace outside of Nashville. Walk around town. You'll see what I mean. Here, take a look at this. You'll like it. Good introduction."

She was a salesman after all. She would not have related to salesperson. I did buy the CD with accompanying book. We did like it. And we did walk around town, what there was of it.

There were two luthiers with beautiful handmade guitars and violins, I mean fiddles, hanging in their windows. One of the shops was in the miniest of mini-malls – an indoor strip mall of sorts. It was there that we entered into a conversation with the only person we saw.

He was sitting in an office with the sign on the window of Floyd County Economic Development Authority. We went in. He was the "Authority." We learned that you can rent space for eight dollars and seventy-five cents a foot a year in the Floyd Innovation Center, which looked to me like a big long barn. I quickly calculated a comparison. One of my first jobs was with a small management consulting firm in Westport, Connecticut. We had about two thousand square feet in downtown Westport. In Floyd dollars that would have cost us seventeen thousand dollars a year. In Westport money that much space would be eighty thousand dollars a year. The Floyd Innovation Center was clearly a bargain.

We learned about attempts to diversify beyond farming and music making. I admit, I sort of liked those two together. We talked more, and the more we talked, the more interesting Floyd became. The more we talked, the more inclined I became to find a place to park Muriel for the night and go listen to some music at one or more of the three restaurants in town. We were assured that they all had music.

Our economic development host said that the local commune, *Abundant Dawn*, might let us park for the night. He knew they let visitors stay. It was ten dollars a night if they provided a bed and food. He guessed they wouldn't charge anything for parking a small RV.

A commune. We had to know more. We asked, and

he told us. Sure enough, there in Floyd, Virginia, was a commune that had been in existence for many years. It currently had ten members and ninety acres. Floyd had a population of only five hundred, so the commune was pretty well known in town. We had a time table though and wanted to get all the way to Ashville before turning around and heading back home by a different route.

Floyd, though, and the Crooked Road. It was one of those places where you leave saying, "Someday I am coming back here and staying a while." I should have sent a thank you note to our waitress. As she had told us, "Interesting place."

Beach Dawn

The gulls shake the night
From their wings
Catching pieces of gold
From the new sun
Lifting slowly in the East.

For a moment all fear is gone
And a joining comes to this
Mystery of morning.

Revenge

"We'll eat at the bar."

She indicated I should sit on the stool to the right of her. "Sit here. That way I won't bump you." There was a martini glass on the bar in front of where she sat. It was half full. Three olives were still on the swizzle stick.

She saw I was puzzled. "I'm left handed."

"Sure," I answered and sat where I was directed.

It was an initial job interview and the two of us were looking past the liquor and glasses on the bar to the Hudson River. There were barges going up and down the waterway. It was November and only a few recreational boats were still out. I knew Pete Seeger had lived someplace up river and had helped make the river clean, or cleaner.

Below, on the bank of the river, were train tracks – the Hudson River Line – that carried thousands of commuters into Manhattan each morning. I wondered if the bar would slip down the hill onto the tracks if it rained for forty days and forty nights. I have no idea why I wondered that.

I thought it was a strange place to conduct an interview for a position in a real estate office, but it was her agency and this is where she wanted to do it. I didn't tell her I found it strange, especially since our lunch interview was at two o clock in the afternoon. I ate a six-inch ham, turkey, and cheese subway in the car on the way down from Connecticut.

The bartender did double duty as waiter. She ordered a salad. I said I wasn't hungry. She gave me a puzzled look. Behind us someplace there must have been a kitchen. We were the only ones at the bar. I couldn't see into the dining rom.

"So, did you have any trouble finding the place?"

"No," your directions were perfect." Actually, I had driven by Sal's Revenge three times before I saw the sign for the bar. She had called it a tavern, and I was expecting something a bit more substantial. We weren't that far away from where I lived in Stamford, Connecticut, and I had allowed myself plenty of time. I thought Sal's Revenge was a strange name for a bar or tavern or whatever it was she wanted to call it.

"I own this place," she said. "It doesn't make any money, so I suppose you could call it a hobby. My father is Sal."

"Does he work with you?"

"Dad? Work? No. He retired years ago. He started the agency. Left it to me."

She paused and took a sip of her martini. "What do you want to drink?"

She motioned to the bartender to come over. I ordered a sparkling water with lime. She continued. "He retired and got out of Dodge, divorcing my mother in the process. Lives in Tucson now. Happy as a clam. He did it all in six months.

"Now he lives in this neat retirement complex with at least a hundred single women for every single man. He doesn't talk about it, but I think he's in Viagra heaven." She drank more of her martini. It was someplace between a slurp and a gulp.

I wondered why she had named the bar after her father. She anticipated my wondering.

"The name? You want to know about the name?"

"It's unique," seemed like a safe response.

"My mother was an alcoholic who was screwing her boss in the insurance agency where she worked. This is where they used to come to get smashed before heading for the sleaze motel down the road. So I bought the place and put dad's name on it to piss her off and to piss on both of them. They're still in town and they have to drive by it every day." Her martini was on its last legs. She sucked an olive off the swizzle stick and swirled the glass with its remnants in the direction of the bartender. Two olives remained.

Why was she telling me all this? I drove all this way for a job interview. I could have been playing golf or spending time going through the New York Times looking for jobs. This was getting weird. I began thinking I should excuse myself and follow Sal's example and get out of Dodge.

Again, she anticipated. "I'm changing the name of the bar."

I didn't say anything. The next martini landed in front of her. She downed the remnants of the first and moved the swizzle stick from the empty glass to the new one.

"From now on it will be Sal and Jenn's Revenge."

Where was this going?

"My about to be ex cheated on me with a fucking twenty-two-year-old who used to be a waitress, excuse me, server, here."

The first martini had kicked in and, given the way she was drinking the second one, it wouldn't be long before the second made an entrance. Her salad arrived.

My left-handed, salad-eating interviewer was Jennnifer Clark of the Clark Real Estate Agency. I had sent her my resume in response to an ad for an office manager. She was tall, late fifties, frosted hair, no chin, and dressed for showing houses. The buttons on her blouse were doing extra duty containing her.

I wanted, no needed, a job. The agency I had been working for in Connecticut had consolidated two offices and since I was the junior of the two office managers I was invited to seek my fortune elsewhere. The company's human resources pimp had uttered the word "redundant" with a smile. Apparently I was not exceptional enough to bump off the older guy who had trained me. My mentor didn't have the good sense to retire, so here I was, dressed in my best and only suit, watching this middle-aged, well-dressed woman inhale martinis in the middle of the afternoon, giving me more information about her family affairs than I had any interest in.

"My ex-husband worked for me. For me. Not with me. For me. The putz. He was my office manager. I fired his ass. His lawyer tried to convince the judge we were partners. Fat chance. The shit. Fired." She enjoyed emphasizing the words "for me" and 'fired."

"So he and miss young tits – did I say she used to work here – are renting a place down the road and he has to commute past here on his way to his job at Home Depot. You've got to love it."

I didn't know what to say, so I finished off my sparkling water and ordered a second. She didn't seem to notice or care that I was not drinking anything alcoholic.

"I need someone to replace him." Her words were starting to lose some of the clenched-jaw precision of the well-educated white WASP.

She turned on her stool to face me. "I checked you out and everyone said you were excellent at your job and had a very good future and were more mature than most people in their early thirties. College degree, too." I didn't correct her that I was only twenty-eight. "They told me you would have gotten the job at the merged office had you had a few more years under your belt. That's what they told me. Said clients liked you." She paused and took another sip. She looked me up and down. "They really liked you. Did you know that?"

I didn't have a chance to respond. She reached over and put her non-martini holding hand on my shoulder. "I want you to replace him. I want you to run the office and this bar as well. I'll give you the usual split at the office and half of any profit you can squeeze out of this place."

Her other hand went up to my other shoulder. Precariously, the martini glass was still in it and I was glad it was almost empty. "Do it for me. Replace the fucker. I guarantee you won't regret it. The office is doing really well and no one has ever paid any attention to the Revenge. It could be a gold mine. Look at this location. The martini hand left my shoulder, swinging towards the window to emphasize the view of the river. Drops of martini mixture flew onto my suit jacket in the process. "Location, location, location. Look at that river." She took another sip and saw the glass was almost empty. She did another swirl towards the bartender and returned her attention to me.

"Treat me right and I'll treat you right and who knows? The sky's the limit. No, there are no limits. You understand. No limits."

I was worried about the reaction of my wife to the smell of alcohol on my jacket. Eight months into marriage, loss of my job, trying to get pregnant, and possibly a move away from her family if I took this job – my cognitive processing was on overload. This lunch interview was much too complex. How much replacement did this woman want? I hated women without chins. I don't know why. I just found them very unattractive.

The ad hadn't mentioned anything about managing anything but a real estate office. I know how to do that. I've done it. Real estate had been my mother's idea. "You're great with people, honey, and there is big money in it. Look at your aunt." Aunt Peg always came up in these discussions. Aunt Peg had not gone to college. Neither had my parents. I had been the first in the family and I had chosen sociology as a major. I had to choose something. Money and a degree in sociology don't go together. I was so broke with student loans that the idea of earning, actually earning "big money" seemed like a fantasy, like wining the lotto. I had a college degree. Aunt Peg didn't. How hard could real estate be? I was tired of moving from bartender to bartender job, interrupted by short spurts of trying things like selling whatevers to whomevers.

In school we had studied the emergence of the "Gig Economy" and its social implications in our course on "Current Social Changes and The Dislocations of the Social Fabric." Anxiety, disconnectedness, and fear of commitment are no longer concepts to me. They were my life before I started in real estate. And now Ms. No Chin was seriously talking to me about managing a bar. Really? Back to a bar.

Aunt Peg, though, the rich one in the family, had made it on her own. Maybe my mother was right. Maybe I could. Nice fantasy. I liked the Lexus Peg drove, and I loved her house. I took an online real estate program. I'm smart enough. I aced all of the tests. I had no trouble getting my sales license. Century 21 hired me and two others for their Stamford office. I became the rentals specialist. "You're young. You can relate to these millennials," proclaimed the office manager. Poof, in one sentence there went my weekends. All day Saturday and every Sunday afternoon I sat at a desk waiting for walk-ins and telephone calls. Once in a while I actually showed someone an apartment. I had lots of time to read trash novels and no time to play golf.

At Christmas dinner, three years out of college and a

year into desk sitting, Aunt Peg, the rich one in the family, told me to get my broker's license as soon as I could because it would give me greater flexibility. She also told me to change agencies. My father argued with his sister. "He needs to stay for a few years or people will say he's a job hopper."

"Stay out of this, Norm. You don't know what you're talking about. Salespeople change agencies all the time."

Just the normal Christmas sibling bickering. He was the oldest so thought he should know more about everything. They loved each other in their bickering way.

In the kitchen, rescued by way of a request to clear the dinner plates, my mother admonished me to listen to my aunt. "Peg is right. As usual, your father doesn't know what he's talking about."

So I got my broker's license. ReMax hired me. I still had no weekends, so when the chance to manage the office came up, I grabbed it, left the "sky's the limit" bullshit of selling, got to play some golf, and Nancy, my elementary teacher fiancée, was a happy camper because it meant we could get chores done on the weekend together. She liked togetherness. Her parents had done togetherness.

And now I had the smell of gin and vermouth on my jacket and chinless Jenn was swirling her way into her third revenge martini. All the olives had disappeared. She reached into her oversized pocketbook which was sitting on the bar and pulled out a manila envelope and handed it to me. "It's all in here. I had my lawyer do it.

Salary, bonuses, health insurance, everything. Take it with you and get back to me tomorrow." She paused and tried to focus on my eyes. "There are no limits," she whispered.

It was clear that the interview was over.

***

I get seasick. In most families that wouldn't matter, but when your father-in-law, brother-in-law, wife, and even your mother-in-law are sailors and compete in races every single weekend from Memorial Day to Labor Day, it matters. Someone should tell advice columnists that you should check out the athletic preferences of a girl's family you are attracted to before you get serious. They all thought I was some kind of lesser being. "How can you get excited about chasing a little white ball all day long. Boring." My argument that twenty-five million people golf, far more than race sailboats, was considered meaningless. It became all about courage and facing danger and racing around the world and on and on. The only place they raced around was buoys in a bay in Long Island Sound. But they talked about round-the-world races and the Americas Cup like they were participants. Thank God we all rooted for the Giants. I never admitted I had once rooted for the Jets. At least they were both New York teams. Nancy's last boyfriend before we got married was a dreaded Boston Patriot's fan.

Sailing is not a cheap sport. Nancy's father could afford it. He could also afford winter vacations to St. Bart's. He could also get off cheap shots about my job as an office manager in a real estate agency rather than being a broker out selling where the "real money" was. His game was advertising. He worked in a big agency and was a partner. He loved the word "partner" and repeated it often.

He commuted daily to Madison Avenue in Manhattan. He brought a big supermarket carton of Pringles home for everybody when he landed the Pringles account. Pringles for God's sake. Selling Pringles was more uplifting than making sure that the sale of people's homes got processed properly, and the office was covered seven days a week, and ads got to the papers when they should. But he made a lot of money selling Pringles.

I don't know what he said to Nancy when I wasn't around about my "prospects." I decided three months ago not to give a shit. I loved Nancy. She was nice to me. She told me to ignore Pringles. She liked teaching and was good at it. She wanted to be a mother and I knew she'd be good at that, too. My mother said I was lucky to have her. I agreed. Nancy didn't notice the smell of gin on my suit jacket when I got home.

That night Nancy and I looked at the papers in chinless Jenn's envelope. "Is this for real?" Nancy asked.

"I think so."

"This is much better than ReMax."

"I know. Salary is better. Benefits are better. And then there is the bar."

"Hon, why would we not do this?"

We had the papers spread out on our bed. Nancy had on a white T-shirt with the logo for the 2012 Caribbean 1600 sailboat race on the front. She hadn't sailed in the race, but her father had helped a friend prepare his boat for the race and had given Pringles, that's what everyone in the family now called him, the T-shirt for helping out. Nancy had spirited the T-shirt away and wore it as a bed shirt, usually by itself, alone, on nights she wanted to have sex. Tonight was an alone night.

"It would mean moving."

"Why? You said it took less than an hour. That's about the same as taking the train into New York."

"It's driving, though, not sitting on the train where you can fall asleep."

She was beginning to case build, and I knew her father would be brought into the conversation at any minute. As if on cue, Pringles made his appearance. "Dad's been doing it for years. It would give you time to think on the way in and decompress on the way back. You couldn't read, but you could listen to books on tape.

"We could stay here. I wouldn't have to change jobs. I like my school. I like my principal. We have friends here. My parents are here. Why would we move?"

I knew the case was a good one, worthy of a smart spouse seeing things her way and creating a litany of reasons why she was right. I tried, though, to generate a counter argument. "It was under an hour mid-day. Not in rush hour traffic."

"What if we tried it for a year?" She squiggled over to where I was sitting on the side of the bed, knelt behind me, and pulled me back into her. Her breasts, sans bra, against my back were always a compelling argument. "If, at the end of a year, it's too much and you like the job and the community, we can move. Hopefully I'll be pregnant by then and would stop teaching anyway."

I know men are somehow supposed to love to drive. Paul Newman, racing cars and all that. The truth, though, is I don't like to drive, especially in the dark and with snow on the ground. I was about to say something when Nancy had the answer already.

"If the weather is really bad some nights you could stay over. Dad does that sometimes if he has an early morning meeting at the office. Just keep a fresh set of underwear, a shirt, and a toiletries kit at your office or at the bar." I had often thought Pringles might have other reasons for his monthly stay-overs but never said anything. No one else did either. And no one seemed to notice that there was a regularity to these early morning meetings. Or, if they noticed, the subject was one more of the family's taboo subjects.

By the time we settled down to some late-night sex, it was all decided. I would call chinless Jenn and accept her offer; we would stay in Stamford – and revisit the topic in a year I kept adding, we would become pregnant in six months (sperm and egg willing), and life would be peachy keen. As Nancy turned off the light she ended with, "If it all goes well and you get that bar really profitable, we could start looking for houses in a year." I didn't dare ask, "Where?" or we never would have gotten to sleep.

***

It was Nancy's idea to drive over with me to see my new office and Sal's Revenge the weekend after I started my new job. It was a cold Saturday but brilliantly clear which brought out shoppers. The going was slow getting out of Stamford and then, driving through White Plains, we were at a crawl. "Is it always like this?" she asked.

"Every morning. Actually, it's worse sometimes." She didn't say anything, and I held back whining or loading on, "I told you so's." I hated the drive twice a day. Half of the time I was in bumper to bumper traffic and it was three hours a day out of my life. I did try listening to books on tape and when I wasn't in traffic I could pay attention. In traffic I was always pushing the back button so I could re-listen to what I had missed. Okay, I admit it. I'm a nervous driver. Did I say I hated driving?

On the other hand, I liked the office. The people were competent and easier to deal with then the Stamford group. Jenn knew what she was doing and trusted me. I found myself having lunch at the Revenge most days. Sometimes Jenn would join me if she didn't have any showings or deals working that needed her attention. The staff of the Revenge, that's what I called it now, was solid. Jenn knew how to hire. All in all, I was a happy camper and the drive was the only major irritation. Nancy had bought me two books on tape and I was doing more reading, or listening, than I had before I started this commuting business, but don't ask me to tell you what I had listened to.

On the way over Nancy and I chatted about both the agency and the tavern – I used that term now. It was an aspiration. After a cursory walk through the real estate office, Nancy said, "Okay. It's a real estate office. Do they really have to all look the same? Is there a special place that makes real estate desks? Are you allowed only one family picture on your desk? Even some of those look made up."

"One of them is."

"What do you mean?"

"Made up. Doris is very pretty, young, and well-endowed. Jenn told me she was always getting hit on so she has a picture of herself on her desk with her older brother and his kids. Cuts down on the hits she says."

"You're kidding."

"That's what she says. I have no idea."

"Jesus. I'm glad a spend my days with third graders. Can we go see the bar?"

"Tavern. The Revenge."

"I thought it was Sal and Jenn's Revenge."

"I'll tell you about it on the way over."

During our drive, Nancy drove, I told her about some of my plans, including diminishing the prominence of Sal and Jenn in the name. "I want to turn it into a place we would want to come to after work. Lots of commuters are getting off the train every night only a half-mile away. I want people to come here for a drink or dinner after work if no one feels like cooking. I want people to conduct business deals here."

"Look at that view," Nancy said when she walked into the dining room.

"It's even better in the bar."

"Oh, hun. This could be a gold mine," she said when she sat down at the bar and looked out over the Hudson. She swiveled around on her stool studying, not saying a word. Then she started: "You need to make it feel like a club where people come to relax after a hard day at work. Like a New York private club. Like…"

I knew where she was going, "Like the Yale Club." Pringles was a Yalie and a member of the Yale Club which was next door to Grand Central Station. He never talked about "the club." It was always the "Yale Club." Boola, boola, Pringles.

"Sort of. You have a better view. Maybe a couple of leather couches and seating arrangements here and there. You could have one couch be a pull out for you when you need to stay over. And the walls desperately need to be painted a different color, and you need some prints of the Hudson. What if all of the prints were by Hudson River School artists? They're romantic, but they'd really fit. And move the big screen over onto the far wall so you don't have to sit at the bar to watch a game and, besides, it's cutting into the view of the river where it is. Right now this place has no personality."

"You're talking about several thousand dollars."

"Not necessarily. Think about it though."

"I like the idea of a club feeling. I'm not sure Jenn will go for laying out the money."

Jenn wasn't against it when I presented it to her the following Monday. "It will be coming out of profits. Your choice," chinless Jenn responded after martini number two when I presented the concept. "Half of it is your money."

I made the changes or, rather, I bought the furniture on Craig's List and had it delivered, arranged for the painting of the bar – Jenn insisted upon using her painter and choosing the color, and the Hudson River School prints were off at the framers. The bartender moved the TV with the help of his cousin and fifty bucks a piece after work one night. I stayed over that night to make sure nothing got broken or stolen and that the TV got put up exactly where I wanted it and, more importantly, that it worked. Fortunately there was already cable there. We added public wi-fi to the list of changes. I also ordered a new sign.

***

Three weeks after Nancy's visit, it began to snow heavily on a Tuesday afternoon. The storm was supposed to have missed the Hudson Valley. It was supposed to have stayed out in the Atlantic. I was supposed to have left early because of the storm. It was clear that none of the supposed to's were going to happen. The sign people were supposed to have been there at four o'clock with the new sign for the Revenge. They didn't make their "supposed to" time.

The new sign would be twice the size of the old one and I had convinced Jenn that a single word, preferably no more than two syllables, should be used for people's about-to-be-favorite watering hole. The names "Sal" and "Jenn" would still appear, but they would be reduced in size compared with the main word, the word customers would identify with, Revenge, as in "Let's meet at the Revenge for a drink."

At first she had just looked at me, "You want to replace the sign. You want to change the name. The new name isn't even up yet. I haven't even gotten to enjoy my ex having to drive by it."

It took some convincing and showing her the corporate identity article in *Bar and Beverage* to bring her around. I had also waited until the third olive had disappeared during our weekly review of Revenge's well-being to show her the article and make my case. She slowly warmed to the idea and when I showed her a sketch for the new sign that I had already had made up, she said, "You're a manipulative little thing aren't you? I like it, though. I like the sign and I like the way you managed me." *Managed me* was a bit slurred. "Sometimes I like being managed. Do you enjoy managing me?"

***

Usually Jenn came to the Revenge only during lunch time. Today, though, she showed up in the late afternoon. I had told her that's when the sign people would be there. She wanted to see it, so she sat at the bar waiting for them while I took care of some odds and ends in the tiny office that I had converted from a storage room. I glanced at my overnight bag in the corner and hoped I wouldn't have to use it tonight.

A few patrons straggled in. Everyone commented on the storm and how bad the driving was getting. By six-thirty there were no more stragglers and I told the bartender, waitress, and cook to go home and I would close up. I told Jenn she could go, too, but she said she wanted to see this "thing."

I left the outside lights on so the sign people would know there were still people there. My every-fifteen-minute call to the sign company kept going to voice mail.

At seven o'clock a truck pulled up in front of the Revenge and two men came in. "We got your sign but there's no way we can put it up in this weather. Too dangerous to be up on the cherry picker with this wind. We're going to leave it right in front…"

"Don't leave it in front; it will get plowed in. Leave it along the side of the building. Can you cover it with tarps or something?"

"It's all wrapped up. Besides, it's going to be out in the weather all the time anyway."

Jenn snickered from the bar. It was the kind of snicker that said, "Stupid."

"Okay," I said. "Be careful, though." He looked at me with pure distain but didn't say anything. I went outside to make sure they put it where I wanted it to stay until they could put it up.

It took them about twenty minutes to unload the sign and put it where I wanted it. They left with a, "See you tomorrow if we can get to you." Not particularly assuring. We already had a sign, though. It had been there for the past two years. Another couple of days wouldn't hurt anything.

I came back into the bar, stamped the snow off my feet, took my coat off, and turned off the outside lights so people would know we were closed. Jenn was sitting at the bar with two martinis in front of her. There were three olives on each swizzle stick. Doesn't look like we're going anyplace tonight. "I'll bartend," she said. "Can you cook?"

"Yes," I said.

"Good. I'll have a steak. Let's jack up the heat in case we lose power.

"You sure you don't want to go home."

"In this shit? Drive a half hour? Not on your life. You're not going anywhere either."

"I need to call my wife."

"Sure. Call your wife." I walked away from Jenn to get some privacy and made my call home.

When I returned to the bar, Jenn greeted me with an outstretched hand holding a martini glass filled to the top. "Here I not only drink em; I make em." She handed me my martini with three olives. "Here's to number one. First sip is always the best."

I took a sip. It was good.

"You like?"

"Yes."

"I made a pitcher."

I took another sip. "Let me start cooking before we lose power." I put the martini down on the bar and headed for the kitchen.

Jenn picked it up and followed me. "Can I use your toothbrush later?" she asked.

Pity the Poor White Man

Pity the poor white man.
One hundred thousand years ago he left
The African Savannah
and traveled north
where white skin worked better than
black skin or brown skin
or any other shade of skin
in the hues of humanity.

Pity the poor white man.
With but for a few lapses in time and place
he has ruled the earth,
and where he didn't rule
he conquered.
He has subjugated women and children;
he has possessed them as he did his cattle.
He has enslaved those with black skin and brown skin;
he has traded them as he did his sheep.

Pity the poor white man.
He didn't ask for change; he didn't plan for change.
He didn't fight for change; he doesn't want change.
He wants to rule, to possess, to enslave.
It's his right, the right of a million years.

Pity the poor white man his angry tantrums,

Pity the poor white man his spasms of fear,
Pity the poor white man;
he no longer has his place.
Pity the poor white man;
he has been the placer.
Pity the poor white man.
One hundred thousand years is a very long time.

First Things First:

First I have to acknowledge her,
Paws up on the bed
Large German Shepherd tongue
Licking me into morning.
I think she operates on light
And I adjust when I go to bed
According to the time of daybreak.
Some insist that it's hunger,
But I have tried feeding her later in the day,
Hoping for another hour's sleep,
But success with this approach
Has never been achieved.
Ignoring her has never worked,
And so I get up, retrieve my blue robe,
The birthday gift I gave myself,
And go downstairs to let her out.

I open the back door to the fenced-in yard
And hope there are no turkeys, coyotes,
Raccoons, foxes, squirrels, or even sparrows
Present to set off a cacophony of barking that
Will wake the neighbors up.

It is my first hope of the day.
There will be other hopes,
Many more as the day passes.

Too many little ones to mention,
Some outside of consciousness,
None large enough to raise to the
Narcissistic level of an "I want,"
Which I tend to reserve
For the people in my life.
But in these miniature hopes
Is the recognition of how small I am.
Within these hopes is
The recognition that I do not control
The wanderings of turkeys and sparrows
And whether my beautiful dog
Will wake the neighbors up.

Freedom and Courage

It was the first week of August. We were together, extended family, to celebrate an anniversary. It was evening and several of us were gathered around the firepit on the edge of the lake. The conversation swirled, as such conversations do, from politics to comparing colleges to family news and quickly in and out of religion which included the statement: "Unitarian Universalism isn't a *real* religion."

Oh, the bait. Oh, the temptation to exclaim, "Yes, it is." But then that would require a rather elaborate explanation of what I thought a *real* religion was and I wasn't about to take that on. The question, though, is an important one. What does constitute a religion?

Stephen Prothero is a professor of religion at Boston University. He wrote a book called *God Is Not One* that tackles that question. The subtitle of his book is: *the eight religions that rule the world and why their differences matter* (Prothero 2010).

Prothero believes that what distinguishes religion from other institutions are the following four characteristics. First, every religion posits a core human problem. Another way of thinking about it is that there is a curse to being human, something about us that causes us problems, something that makes us less than angelic. For example, in Christianity the core problem is sin. In Islam it is pride. In Buddhism it is suffering. If Unitarian Universalism is a *real* religion, what do

Unitarian Universalists (UU) think is the problem or curse of being human? What is the core human problem?

Second, every religion comes up with a response to its understanding of the core human problem. Every religion says: we have the solution. For Christians the solution is salvation. For Muslims it is submission to the will of Allah. For Buddhists it is enlightenment. What is the solution that UUs offer? It is hard to come up with a solution if you don't know what the problem is.

Third, according to Prothero, every religion offers a technique, sometimes several, for getting this solution to work for you. For Christians it is prayer and good works. For Muslims it is the four pillars: prayer, charity, fasting, and pilgrimage. For Buddhists it is meditation and the eight-fold path. And the technique of Unitarian Universalism is? Ooops. Without a problem or a solution, it is tough to have techniques. Perhaps the seven principles that Unitarian Universalists hold dear might fit here, but they are not really techniques. They are closer to an ethical stance, and it is a stance that many religious groups would also subscribe to. In Unitarian Universalism there is an agreement among the congregations, a covenant, to affirm seven ethical principles:

We, the member congregations of the Unitarian Universalist Association, covenant to affirm and promote"

The inherent worth and dignity of every person;

Justice, equity and compassion in human

relations;

Acceptance of one another and encouragement to spiritual growth in our congregations;

A free and responsible search for truth and meaning;

The right of conscience and the use of the democratic process within our congregations and in society at large;

The goal of world community with peace, liberty, and justice for all;

Respect for the interdependent web of all existence of which we are a part.

Fourth, every religion has exemplars. These are the models who chart the path for us. Catholics emphasize saints and families give their children the names of saints at Baptism. My parents gave me the name Vaughn *Francis* Keller. When I was confirmed in the Catholic Religion, I chose Francis as my confirmation name. St. Francis of Assisi is not a bad exemplar. Unitarian Universalism does have its heroes. Channing, Parker, and Fahs might qualify. Are these, exemplars, though? In addition, these are the names of religious insiders and their stories are not well known, even among UUs.

So, how does a Unitarian Universalist sitting around a firepit take the bait? There is the duck and cover strategy: as UUs we are free to create our own religion. But then the questioner says, "Okay, what do *you* think the curse is, and what is *your* solution, what are *your* techniques, and who are *your* exemplars?" Oops. Is this where the UU retreats to the seven principles which are really an ethical system that is similar to that of every progressive religion today? Or does the UU create a masterpiece of appropriation, borrowing a little bit of Buddhism mixed in with a tablespoon of paganism, and spice it with a touch of Daoism without ever really struggling to articulate the four elements?

I am a UU. So, what might I have answered had I been so inclined and had sufficient time? It is not easy because UUs, as a denomination, are so committed to our "liberalness." We don't have any sacred texts other than our seven ethical statements. So we have to go it alone but do so in community. Maybe that is our curse as a denomination. But beyond our own particular problem as a denomination, what is the curse of humankind, what is your problem and mine?

I believe it is freedom. We, as a species, are cursed with freedom. We are free. We are free to sin. We are free to wallow in pride. We are free to cause suffering. I remember the first time I fully understood this. It was during a break in a summer school graduate class. It was our dinner break, and I was sitting on a hill with others overlooking the campus. There was a chatty conversation going on about me and I zoned out. There was an ant starting to crawl up over my sneakers heading towards my leg. I could shake it off, brush it out, swat it, or ignore it. I could do any of those things. I was free to choose. Whatever I did, though, I was responsible. Was I Schweitzer? Did the ant get to live? I swished it away. Not a gentle Schweitzer swish, but at least a swish rather than a swat.

We are incredibly free to cheat, steal, zone out, and on and on. I believe freedom is our curse. We are free to be cynical, joyous, engaged, or distant. We can be loving or a bully.

What, though, when things are truly desperate and what we often think of as freedom has been taken away from us? This is the question that Viktor Frankl confronted in writing *Man's Search for Meaning* (Frankl 1946). His answer: we are always free to choose our attitude towards even the desperate depravity of the holocaust. People were confined, tortured, mutilated, and forced to watch loved one be killed: minute by minute horrors. Yet, in the midst of this, some people were creative, compassionate, and engaged fully with life. Freedom is our gift and our problem.

We can run away from freedom. That is one solution to the curse. Erich Fromm addresses this in his book *Escape From Freedom* (Fromm 1941). This book came from observations of what was happening in Germany as it marched towards the second world war.

Fromm addresses three negative responses we can have to our freedom. This is how we can escape from our curse. None of these are solutions. These are the perversions of a solution. These are escape routes we can take to avoid confronting freedom.

He explicates these mechanisms in the fifth chapter of the book. He writes, "The first mechanism of escape from freedom I am going to deal with is the tendency to give up independence of one's own individual self and to fuse one's self with somebody or something outside oneself in order to acquire the strength which the individual self is lacking."

He describes the various ways we can adopt an authoritarian response to escape from the curse of freedom: the curse of being responsible, thoughtful, truly engaged in our life. He describes how we can do it by fusing with another person, perhaps in a misguided love. We can do it with an idea like the writings of Ayn Rand. We can create a hero and bestow an unmitigated trust in the person. Essentially, we surrender critical thinking and critical judgment once we have made these commitments. But, there is a payoff. Our need to belong is satisfied. We are connected. We belong to this person or this group. We no longer feel the unbearable feelings of powerlessness and separateness. We have escaped from freedom.

Destructivness is the second way in which we can escape from freedom. Here we do not enter into a symbiotic relationship. We, instead, try to destroy what it is that we believe is contributing to our experience of powerlessness. To make it acceptable and suppress our conscience we can call it love, duty, patriotism, etc. We will, however, destroy the other or others in order to regain a sense of power. The destructiveness will reduce the anxiety I experience. It will reduce by aloneness when I do it with others. Think of gangs. Think of war. Destroy, destroy, destroy that which makes us feel alone. Destroy that which makes us feel powerless.

Or I can escape from freedom by becoming an

automaton sleepwalking through life, following all of the social signs that tell me what to do and when to do it. I have been handed a book of thou shalt nots and I shall by my parents and by society. I shall not steal. But I never question why. I shall have children, but why? I can escape freedom by a constant striving to be normal. My drive is to be "normal." I escape freedom by uttering the prayer, "Please god, let me be normal." When things are anything but normal, I reshape them to make them appear normal. The child of an alcoholic often learns how to do this. The child says, "I don't have to think about the fact that my mother is an alcoholic. I don't want to think about it." I escape from freedom by dulling my perceptions and feelings and sleepwalking through my life. I want the world to see me and my family as normal. So, I become an automaton. If I wonder once in a while about confronting my reality, I suppress it and will use "obligations" as a rationale for why I am not free. But, in fact, I am free; I just can't bear it.

So, if freedom is the problem, the curse, what is the solution offered by my religion? Please note: mine rather than Unitarian Universalism. For me it is contained in the title of another book. Paul Tillich wrote, *The Courage to Be* in 1952 (Tillich 1952). As an aside, the introduction to the edition I have was written by none other than the Reverend Peter Gomes of Plymouth, Massachusetts.

I believe that the solution to the problem of freedom is courage. The kind of courage I am speaking of, though, is not the courage of the hero who is reactive and rushes into a fire to save a child. This is a heroic act. In the Ken Burns Lynn Novick video series *Viet Nam*, there are many acts of heroism depicted in the films. To a person, though, these heroes talk about their reactivity. "I just did it."

Existential courage, the kind that Tillich speaks of, is of a different kind. It looks freedom and anxiety straight in the face. It is thoughtful. It accepts the possibility of embarrassment or threat. Doubt is experienced as natural. "The dark night of the soul" is embraced. In Tillich's language, it is the courage to take on the anxiety of meaninglessness. Tillich believes that the courage to be is an affirmation of being versus non-being.

The writings of Fromm, Frankl, and Tillich follow similar paths. Fromm says the meaning of life is to live and that when we escape freedom we are not living. This affirmation of life and full engagement with life, though, takes courage. Anxiety, fear, confronts us. Rather than escaping from freedom, the courage to be means embracing it. Tillich uses the word God but turns it on its head. He writes: "The courage to be is rooted in the God who appears when God has disappeared in the anxiety of doubt (p190)." There is a faith here. It is a mystical expression. I believe it is faith in courage itself.

Just as we can run away, escape from freedom, so we can choose non-being over being. We can choose not to be courageous. We all know the ways in which we can do this, either periodically or on an ongoing basis. Some of these overlap with how we can escape from freedom.

- I may deny what I am seeing or hearing. I may identify with the person, or group, or culture that is causing me or those I love distress. The bonds may be strong, perhaps loving. "The police will protect you." "Americans are good people." "A teacher would never do that." "A priest would never do that." "The president (who I voted for) would never lie to me like that."

- I may minimize the situation by focusing on the good things that a person or culture or group is known for. Or I think in terms of a "few bad apples" rather than the system that creates and supports the bad apples.

- I can use my life, my busyness, as a filtering system that does not allow negativity to penetrate the bubble I have created. As the wicked witch sings in the musical *The Wiz,* "Don't bring me no bad news." I turn away from or turn off information that might distress me. I become a horse wearing blinders racing down the narrow path of my life, unable to absorb or acknowledge the reality of others or of my own situation. If I let it in, I might feel I have to do something about it.

- I may accept the harm as a natural phenomenon: "it is what it is." This "harm" is hardwired into existence, and I can cite proof for this premise. It's just who I am or just who they are.

- I might have to acknowledge my own

culpability, my own participation in the creation or maintenance of the evil or harm. I can't tolerate this guilt. I avoid the reality by re-framing the reality, or re-framing my relationship to it. I create a scenario in which I emerge as a good person, a person I can tolerate. Me and my party or organization are all on the side of the angels.

• I may tell myself the odds against success are too great: They will never change. I will never change. I retreat from engagement with the harm being done. I accept the status quo as the best we can ever hope for.

• I may empathize with the perpetrators. "There are always two sides to every story." The difficulty, of course, is in being able to both empathize with the perpetrators when justified and to have the courage to confront the behavior that is harmful to the victims.

I think this framework of freedom and courage is consistent with the traditions of both Unitarians and Universalists. I believe, as humans, we are cursed with freedom. But I believe there is a solution. I believe it is courage. I believe there are techniques suggested by this framework that are not terribly unique, and I am delighted to borrow my exemplars from wherever I can find them.

I think a firepit is a wonderful place to discuss religion. Maybe next time.

References

Frankl, V. (1946). <u>Man's search for meaning</u>. Boston, Beacon Press.

Fromm, E. (1941). <u>Escape fom freedom</u>. New York, Farra & Rinehart Books.

Prothero, S. (2010). <u>God is not one</u>. New YOrk, Harper One.

Tillich, P. (1952). <u>The courage to be</u>. New Haven, CT, Yale University Press.

Friends and Fireworks

The next wish rises to a pause
and flings its bronze fingers
out against the sky.

My children come in close
for warmth against the night
using up another hope
that I can body-back
all harm from them.

Next blue, white, and red circles whistle down
ending in three sharp bangs
      that jolt us tight each time.

Around me friends lie still between assaults
allowed by the sharing of robes
to gently touch, enfold each other
in this annual rite.

And then it ends and the rush begins
to our private snails
we inch with so much patience home
with yawned critiques
anticipating sleep.

Words Work

Words have worked for me.
They always have.
By contrast, and failure,
The symbiology of numbers,
And letters and numbers together,
Never caught my imagination and
My imagination failed to decode their meanings.

So I left mathematics and laboratories to others
Who found meaning in what to me was a mess
Of unfamiliarity beyond my ability
and interest
and willingness
to invest my ignorance.

Words, though, words worked for me.
The parsing was acceptable though tedious.
But words. These symbols, ah, these symbols,
Unlike those of the equation and the microscope,
Words spoke to my imagination
And my imagination reached out and understood
that a whale was evil, even though it was white,
and an old man could dream of young lions
playing on a beach and find peace.

Words worked for me at work
Spinning out theories and rationales
In memos that some people

Read and transformed into action.
Words worked for me, sometimes well, sometimes not,
in poems and stories
and essays and even
the marathon of the novel.

Words worked for me in the privacy of my journal
recording and probing,
deceiving and revealing.

And then they stopped.

Age, regrets, simple pleasures, chaos, awareness,
and I simply don't know what
other than that they stopped.

It is easy to lie with words, too easy to lie with words.
Politicians word their way into power.
Lovers word their way away from love.

And authors. Authors lie all the time,
Except for the great ones,
The DiMaggio's of words.

Words no longer work for me.
Words no longer clothe me.
I come more naked, now, into experience.
Wordless, as I approach death.
I come naked now.

Words no longer work for me,
But at times they are all I have.

Consuela Maria Has the Flu

Mickey

It was going to be a bad day. Customers at the airport were calling and calling again. Annoyance was escalating into anger and then outrage. The *Close Park* bus hadn't made a loop in more than thirty minutes to pick up people from their airline terminals and take them to the *Close Park* office where their cars were. At the office, it was crowded. Customers were sitting and standing in the waiting room.

"I'm going to miss my flight. Where's the bus?" became the chorus in a bad song to Mickey's ears. Only one bus was running and it was tied up in traffic.

Consuela Maria getting the flu started it all. She had been one of Mickey Simpson's bus drivers for three years and had never missed a day of work. Mickey was surprised, then, when Consuela Maria's daughter called and left a message on his cell phone telling him that her mother was very sick. The daughter reported in detail that her mother had been throwing up and had a fever. Mickey called their house when he came in to start his shift and asked if Consuela Maria was okay and the daughter said she would be. They were private people and Mickey didn't push. Dependable drivers were hard to find and Consuela Maria was his most dependable driver. She was the only driver who had been with *Close*

Park since Mickey and his brother had taken out second mortgages on their homes so they could buy the business three years ago.

Mickey was already down one driver because of the damned flu. His own wife was just getting over it, and he was hoping that he would not be next. "Next year everyone gets the flu shots if I have to pay for them myself," he said to Keisha who took the calls and was his cashier. He knew he wouldn't, and he doubted that his employees would get the shots. They were part-timers and most of them didn't have health insurance. Some didn't even have a doctor.

Chris

The traffic seemed extra heavy. Monday morning. It had only been four months and Chris had forgotten how bad the morning traffic was between Rockland and Boston. He thought he had left enough time, but he hadn't been thinking too straight since he was laid off. Seventeen weeks. Only one week left before his severance was finished. One week for every year he had worked. It sounded like a lot when they first told him.

It was a big bakery, but it was a family business and "Junior" had just completed his MBA at Northeastern and needed a job. Even with an MBA, jobs were hard to find, and Junior didn't look too hard. Chris didn't have an MBA. That never seemed to matter until Junior had his. Being chief financial officer of a bakery wasn't all that complicated, and the two sisters and their mother who owned the bakery had always seemed happy with

Chris's work. But Junior had to be taken care of. Chris pledged once more that this was the last time he would work for a family business.

He glanced again at his GPS and his anxiety went up a few notches as he saw how long it was going to take him before he got to *Close Park*. The traffic was crawling on Route 93, inching its way towards Boston and Logan Airport.

Sixteen weeks of internet searching, newspaper reading, friend calling, resume sending, and dressing every morning as though he was going for work the way the *Job Hunter's Guide* suggested, and he had not gone on a single interview. Nothing. Worse than nothing. Everyone he talked to told him that there were no prospects for anything changing. He was done, finished at the age of thirty-nine. Done. A divorced man with two about-to-be teenagers; he had child-support payments and a rented one-bedroom apartment with a pullout couch in the living room. His ten-year-old car had close to two hundred thousand miles on it and needed a new transmission. His sister had sent him the airplane ticket for Chicago, but he would have to pay for the parking at *Close Park*. Her husband would pick him up at O'Hare Airport when he got to Chicago.

Jan

The pain surprised her. People had told her about it, but this was her first operation and she didn't know. The fatigue surprised her. She had been told about that as well, but she was in good shape thanks to her Jazzercise classes and thought people were overdoing it with their warnings. Besides, she was needed at work.

The surgery itself had come as a surprise. The fibroids had grown quickly, as had the discomfort. It made the decision to have the hysterectomy easy. Having her first child at forty-one, her gynecologist told her she was technically referred to as a "senile mother." He thought it was funny. She didn't. He said they didn't know if her being a "senile mother" had increased the risk of her "runaway" fibroids, as he called them. She didn't care. There was nothing she could do about her age.

She and Norm had argued about calling Chris: "You're not making sense, Jan. He's not working. You know damned well he'll come if we ask him."

"He's never taken care of a three-year-old and a five-year-old by himself." As she said it, she knew Norm was right.

"He won't be taking care of the kids alone. You'll be right here in the house with him."

It was hard for her to argue with that. Still, the idea of relying on her kid brother didn't sit well with her. She knew she was still angry at Chris for screwing up his marriage, and she suspected his losing his job wasn't just because this "Junior" needed a job.

But Norm was right: they needed help for a couple of weeks, Norm couldn't take any more time off from work, she was too weak to take care of the kids, Chris wasn't working, and he had even offered. Basically, Chris was pretty reliable. So it was settled.

Chris

He wasn't going to make it. He knew it as he drove by the Logan turn off and worked his way down Route 1 towards *Close Park*, which wasn't feeling very close. Shit. Norm would be waiting for him at O'Hare. He hadn't looked to see when the next flight was. No matter what, he'd have to pay a change fee and he was already close to the limit on his credit card. Another failure. He should have known. He tried to take a deep breath, but couldn't quite do it. He was on the edge of tears and he hated that feeling. It had happened too often in the two years since Marcy had told him she wanted a divorce. That he was the one who had worked ridiculous hours and was never home didn't matter. He didn't want to get divorced. When he thought about the reasons for the divorce, he always focused on the long hours that Marcy complained about. He couldn't help the traffic to and from Boston. They were always ten-hour days and sometimes twelve. He couldn't help that. He avoided thinking about his affair with the dispatcher. Marcy had found out some, but not all, of that story.

He got off of Route 1 and pulled into *Close Park* just as one of their buses was pulling in over the spiked grate that only let you drive one way without blowing out your tires. Great, he thought, quick turn around and I'll be on the next bus. He didn't notice the two parked buses at the edge of the lot.

He parked in front of the office, brought his keys with him, and went to the valet desk. He was surprised at all of the people in the waiting room. Some of them had seen the bus coming in and were brushing by him to be the first in line to get on.

Keisha was sitting behind her computer and asked, "Do you have a reservation?" He said he did. "Name?" He provided it. A couple of key strokes later she asked for his credit card. He handed it to her; she swiped it, waited for the receipt to print out, handed it to him with a pen, and smiled at him. Chris wasn't smiling. The bus was filling up and Mickey was already announcing: "We'll have another bus in a couple of minutes folks." Mickey knew he wouldn't, but he didn't know what else to say. He couldn't very well say, "Sorry, folks. Consuela Maria has the flu and you may miss your flight."

Chris heard the bus start to leave as he reached down to pick up the handle on his roll-a-board suitcase. The "shit" wasn't quite under his breath. "Sorry," Keisha said. "The bus will be back soon."

"I left too late. Damned traffic."

"It's bad Monday morning. Where you going?"

"Chicago."

"Business?"

Hearing her ask that, he felt embarrassed. "No. Going to take care of my niece and nephew for a while. My sister's sick."

"That's nice. Not that she's sick. That you're going to help out."

"Thanks." Chris smiled at her affirmation. Keisha was smiling back. Chris's smile got a little bigger. Chris looked at his watch. There was no way he was going to make his flight. "Excuse me. I've got to call my sister and tell her I've missed my flight."

"Sorry."

Conor

Conor was having a hell of a hard time keeping his eyes open. He hadn't slept in close to twenty hours, but with Consuela Maria out, Mickey told him he had no choice but to drive today. Connor had been on as night manager until Mickey showed up at seven, and now he had to drive. He had protested, but even though he and Mickey were brothers and owned *Close Park* together, Mickey was still the big brother and he also owned more of *Close Park* than Conor did. So he drove. Traffic was starting to thin out which made it easier. He did better when he was moving. When he got stuck in traffic his eyes started to close.

The light was orange, but he knew he could make it and he wanted to keep moving. He hated stopping now. Now it was red, but it had only been red for a couple of seconds and he didn't see anyone coming. The driver of the old Buick pulling out of the gas station on the corner had the same idea and was sure the *Close Park* bus was going to stop. The driver was surprised, then, when he heard the crashing sound and felt his car lurch forward as the *Close Park* bus pushed him through the intersection like he was on a pool table and the pool stick had just launched him towards the far pocket.

His seat belt held him in place and the crash wasn't strong enough to set off his airbag. He seemed okay. He checked again and concluded he was okay and he should get out of the car to see what had happened.

Things were not that calm on the bus. Without seat belts, and with several people standing because Conor had filled the bus to its limit, people and suitcases were thrown all over. There were several cries of pains as elbows, suitcase corners, and bodies fell on top of one another. "Get off me." "I can't breathe." "Hon, are you alright?" were mixed with expletives and a young girl and her brother crying.

Conor pulled on the handle to open the front door of the bus. It wouldn't move. The bus's right fender had been pushed back, jamming it closed. He'd have to get to the back window and pop it open, but that would mean crawling over people and the suitcases that had been thrown all over the bus. Conor pushed the button again to open the door. It didn't move. He put his head down between his arms on the steering wheel and just started swearing and banging his hands on the wheel. All he could think of were lawsuits, losing the business, and not being able to pay the second, or even the first, mortgage on the house because everything was now invested in the business.

Meanwhile, people were screaming, "Let us out of here." He undid his seat belt and went to the door and tried to push it open. It wouldn't move. People kept shouting, "Let us out of here." Conor didn't know how to do that. He'd like to. He had tried opening the door.

Damn it. They could see he was trying. It wouldn't open. They were trapped inside the bus. It wouldn't be long. But for now, they were trapped. He took out his cell phone.

Mickey

"You're in charge," Mickey whispered in Keisha's ear as he grabbed the keys for one of the buses at the end of the parking lot. "Conor's been in an accident and I've got to get down there and pick those people up. Tell these people we're sorry, but they'll have to go park someplace else or take cabs. Give them a voucher for a day of free parking any time they want."

"I could lock up and drive the people who are here."

"Without a commercial license? No way. We've got enough troubles."

Mickey was out the door and trotting towards one of the empty buses. He hadn't meant for Keisha to use the loudspeaker system, but she did. As he approached the bus he heard her on the outside speaker: "We're sorry, but there has been an accident and we will not be able to take you to the airport. We will give you a voucher for a free day of parking."

Chris

Chris laughed. He couldn't help himself. The woman standing next to him looked at him strangely before she asked him what he was laughing at.

"I've lost my job, gotten divorced, my sister's sick, I'm trying to get to Chicago to help her with her kids, and now I've missed my plane. I'm broke, and now I have to pay for a cab to get me to airport where I get to pay the airlines a change fee. Laugh or cry. Laughing seems to be a slightly better choice."

She became firm: "I'm going to drive over and see if I can park in general parking at the airport. You can come with me. It will save you the cab fare."

Chris saw she was serious and trying to get him to be serious. He calmed down. "Thank you." He looked at her. Gray hair. Probably in her late fifties. Professionally dressed. A little chunky. Take-charge kind of person. "Sorry for the outburst. It's been a rough day so far."

She didn't respond to his apology. "Shall we go?"

"Can I help you with your bag?" he asked, trying to impress her with his politeness.

"I've got it." She clearly did not need his help.

"My name's Chris, Chris Jameson."

She didn't acknowledge his name. She simply walked over to Keisha, retrieved her keys and the voucher for a free day of parking, and walked out of the office expecting him to follow her, which he did.

Chris liked cars. He had wealth fantasies about them. He had a lot of those lately. Her car was a new BMW 750Li xDrive sedan with dealer plates. She used her key to open the doors, start the car, and open the trunk. Without a word, they put their luggage in the trunk and climbed into their respective seats for passenger and driver.

They exited the parking lot and immediately were caught up in the backup from the accident. She did a U-turn and headed in the opposite direction. "I know how to get around this mess," she said.

"Great." Chris answered. "Nice car. New?"

"It's one of our demos."

"You work for a dealership?"

"I own three: one in Plymouth, one in Duxbury, and one in Hingham."

"Really?"

"Really. Surprised?"

"I guess."

"I operated them with my late husband. When he died I just kept on running them the way I did when he was alive."

"Oh. Sorry about your husband."

She ignored his comment. "I've got a Toyota–Lexus franchise in Plymouth, Volkswagen-BMW in Duxbury, and Honda-Infiniti in Hingham."

"Wow."

"Yes, wow."

"Tough business."

"Not really. We have almost no influence over the manufacturers, so it's all in location, employees, margins, and advertising. Employees are the most troublesome. The sales people are migrant workers and the techs are prima donnas."

"You hire migrant workers to sell?"

"That's what they are. They bounce from dealership to dealership looking for the best situation. If a car's hot, that's where they want to be. If the sales manager plays loose with the owner's margins, they love the sales manager. If the sales manager hangs tough, they hate him.

"Money's in service, anyway. Techs are like little babies, but at least they stay around if you treat them well. What do, or did, you do?"

Chris felt judged. "I was the finance manager for *Bread in the Hub* bakery. Names supposed to be a double entendre or something. You know them?"

"Yes. How long?"

"Seventeen years."

"Really?" Now she sounded surprised. "What happened?"

Chris told her the story of Junior and his MBA. "MBA is over rated. Doesn't give you common sense."

Chris didn't answer.

"You're divorced."

"Yes." Chris surprised himself with what happened next, but he felt like he didn't have a choice. "I was stupid and had an affair."

"Kids?"

"Two."

"Child support?"

"Yes." He found himself giving one-word answers. She didn't seem to want more than that.

"Up to date?"

"On what?"

"Child support payments."

"Of course."

"How old are your sister's children?"

"Three and five."

"How long will you be in Chicago?"

"Two weeks."

They had reached the garage for general parking and were slowly circling up the ramp looking for a parking place. They reached the top without finding one and started the downward spiral. Two floors later they saw a car pulling out. They pulled in. She turned the car off and reached in her purse and took out a business card. She handed it to Chris.

"Take this. Call me when you get back. It's time for my finance guy to retire. We've talked about it, but he hasn't made up his mind yet. He's my brother-in-law, so I can't very well push. I want to get someone on board as both a replacement and an encouragement. I'm not offering you a job. I'm offering you an interview when you get back. You seem to stay around and follow through on commitments. You interested?"

"Yes. Thank you."

"Good. Call me when you know your return plans and we'll set up a time to come in."

"Thank you."

Consuela Maria

It had been a week and a half since she had gotten back to work. She was feeling fine now, although she still felt a bit more tired than usual.

Mickey was still fretting and hyper about everything. No one was hurt in Conor's accident, and all that happened was Conor got a ticket for going through a red light and the right fender had to be replaced and insurance paid for most of that. Mickey had given everyone on the bus a week's worth of free parking, had convinced the cop to let him drive them to the airport, and had made sure that he picked them up himself when he knew when they were coming in. He was still a nervous wreck though.

She knew Mickey didn't blame her for the accident, but sometimes he acted weird with her, like he did blame her. Keisha told her that he'd get over it even though every once in a while Mickey said, "If only Maria hadn't gotten the flu." He never called her by her full name, or even Consuela, no matter how often she had asked him to. It was always Maria, never Consuela Maria. So she stopped asking.

It was Keisha's day off, so it was Mickey who called her with the numbers for her next pick up. She had one at the American Airlines terminal. Mickey forgot to give her the name. "Name?" she asked.

"Jameson," he answered. "Chris Jameson."

Pittsburgh Airport

Been doing it for years and years,
This traveling all alone.
I know the airport names by heart –
The miles and miles I've flown.

B.O.S . and D.C.A.
O.R.D. and M.I.A.
L.A.X. and O.M.A.
A.T.L. and J.F.K.

It's the Pittsburgh airport now
And I'm looking for a meal.
The sign outside this door
Says they've got a super deal.

I go right in and look about
And see it still again,
The tables set for two and four –
I'm one, there are no more, no more.

Robin rode in Batman's car
Lois Lane loved Superman
Robin Hood had Little John
And Kirk with Spock explored the stars.

I sit right down and order up

The special's nice and tame
It's cheap, it's plain, per diem type,
My bosses won't complain.

A.N.C. and E.U.G.
C.L.E. and A.L.B.
I.S.P. and C.R.P.
E.R.I. and A.B.E.

But in my daydream world
I think the same old thing
This traveling all alone
Will never make me sing.

Robin rode in Batman's car
Lois Lane loved Superman
Robin Hood had Little John
And Kirk with Spock explored the stars.

But then a tinny voice
Comes whining down the hall
Flight sixty-four to Wichita
Is closing up the door.
Oh no! It's eight, I'm late.
I've dropped the ball once more.

So back to dreams I go
And play my silly game
Of wishing it could be
That voice had called my name

And said,

Come, Kemo Sabe,
We must go
Silver is saddled
We must go
The outlaws are fleeing
We must go
They're depending on us
We must go

Robin rode in Batman's car
Lois Lane loved Superman
Robin Hood had Little John
And Kirk with Spock explored the stars.

Wait, the voice did call my name.

Come, Kemo Sabe,
We must go
Silver is saddled
We must go
The outlaws are fleeing
We must go
They're depending on us
We must go.
We must go
We must go
And so I go.

Vaughn F. Keller

Vaughn Keller has been a police officer, high school teacher, launch boy, university professor, boat captain, researcher, salesman, psychotherapist, bartender, and consultant. Through it all he has written: short stories, professional articles, essays, poetry, and novels. Along the way he has collected two masters degrees, a doctorate, three professional certificates, and more graduate credits than anyone should ever have.

He lives in Plymouth, Massachusetts with a sprightly Cockapoo, Jake.

When not writing he can be found sailing, traveling, or taking out the garbage. He can be reached at vfkeller@gmail.com.